Pride Publishing books by Peter E. Fenton

Single Books
The Woodcarver's Model

The Declan Hunt Mysteries
Mann Hunt
Hoodoo House

The Declan Hunt Mysteries

HOODOO HOUSE

PETER E. FENTON

Hoodoo House
ISBN # 978-1-80250-732-4
©Copyright Peter E. Fenton 2024
Cover Art by Erin Dameron-Hill ©Copyright June 2024
Interior text design by Claire Siemaszkiewicz
Pride Publishing

Published in 2024 by Pride Publishing, United Kingdom.

Pride Publishing is an imprint of Totally Entwined Group Limited.

HOODOO HOUSE

Dedication

For my sister, Carol

Prologue

Mrs Cameron stood at the kitchen sink, considering the dishes created by her morning baking. She stared at the boarded-up kitchen window, the result of a strong dust devil that had hit the north side of the house and torn off a section of the roof a week ago. A sheet of plywood shielded the glass from the repair work above on the decaying one-hundred-and five-year-old wood-framed house.

With the light from the outside cut off, the windowpane became a dim mirror reflecting the activity and inhabitants of the kitchen. Mrs Cameron looked at her reflection and saw a woman with a jowly countenance and hair that had gone completely white. She hadn't turned full-on apple doll yet, but it was inevitable — unless, of course, death took her first.

When did you become so old?

Her thoughts were interrupted.

"What's this symbol called?" Henry asked, holding up a piece of paper and pointing to an indiscernible character. He was surrounded by the remains of his math homework spread all over the table.

"Well, you're gonna have to bring it here. My eyes aren't telescopes."

Henry scooted the chair back, brought her the paper and held it up to her milky blue eyes. She pulled her reading glasses out of the pocket of her apron and held them in front of her, like a jeweller would hold their loupe while examining a rare gem.

"It's a pi," she said.

"I like pie," he said with a smile.

She raised an eyebrow. "Now how long have you been waiting to tell that joke?"

"It's not so much a joke as witty wordplay," he said, heading back to his chair.

This from a thirteen-year-old, she thought, shaking her head. Henry often seemed wiser than a boy of his age. Although he was only her ward, she thought of him as the child she'd never had and due to their age difference, he had taken to calling her Gramma Carol.

She patted him on the shoulder. "Now, clear up your mess and set the table. Then you can go and tell Mr Tull breakfast is ready."

Henry quickly did as he was told.

Mrs Cameron smiled as she looked around. The kitchen was her domain and nobody in Hoodoo House would dare to question anything she did here or, frankly, anywhere else on the property. She was the housekeeper, cook, scullery maid and holder of just about every other staff position one could imagine. She was as permanent a fixture in the building as the ancient stove or the kitchen's large wooden prep table and she loved every scrap of wood and broken-down fixture in it...almost as much as she loved young Henry.

Writer Malcolm Tull, however…

An acrid smell hit her nostrils.

"Damn."

She ran towards the oven. A cloud of smoke filled the air as she pulled out the tray of burnt baking.

"You damned fool," she muttered to herself as she removed the biscuits and placed them on a cooling rack. She could scrape the char off the best ones and they'd be fine. The others she'd save for crumbling up for the chickens, or perhaps the centres could be used for stuffing. Either way, they would end up inside a chicken.

She checked the coffee perking in the pot and dabbed the fat off the freshly cooked bacon. She turned back towards the kitchen table and was startled to see Henry standing at the door, his eyes wide, his mouth open. It took him a moment to speak.

"There's something wrong with Mr Tull."

"Well, what's wrong?" she asked.

"He's asleep on his desk and he's lying in his own sick."

Mrs Cameron hurried to the writing room. Henry followed. She went to the desk and examined the prone man. She'd been around long enough to know when something wasn't alive, but to be certain, she checked for a pulse — nothing.

"Henry, leave the room and don't touch anything. And don't come back in here."

She scurried past the boy and headed back to the kitchen where she called the doctor…and the police.

* * * *

Sergeant Kaci Bowen from the Drumheller, Alberta RCMP detachment was in her late fifties and moved like she'd walked too many miles in cheap shoes. She trudged into the writing room. It was a large space with bookshelves on three walls and a sizeable casement window in the fourth which faced the roadway and the distant fields of prairie grass beyond. As had been reported, the body of writer Malcolm Tull, forty-five years old, was seated in a leather chair behind an expansive oak desk. His torso, head and arms lay across the desk. His face lay in a pool of vomit, which had formed a ring around a blue ceramic coffee mug just beyond reach of Tull's right hand. On the left side of the desk was a prescription bottle one-third full of round white tablets.

Sergeant Bowen walked behind the desk and craned her head over the rigid body, noting that the pill bottle's label identified the contents as primidone, prescribed to Malcolm Tull.

"Is he dead?" a voice asked from the doorway.

Sergeant Bowen looked up and saw a teen-aged boy with tousled mouse-brown hair. She guessed he was a hundred and fifty-six, maybe fifty-seven centimetres tall, and forty-five kilos, tops. She was good at guessing heights and weights. When she retired, maybe she'd join a sideshow.

"You shouldn't be in here," she said.

She walked the boy out into the hallway. *No point in him spending any more time than necessary around the dead body*. The officer looked more closely at the teen. He wore a long-sleeved plaid shirt, jeans and high-top runners. If it wasn't for the shoes, the kid could have been a farm hand. There were plenty just like him all across Wheatland County.

"Henry, isn't it?" she said.

"Yes, ma'am. Henry Quill," he answered, bowing his head and avoiding eye contact.

She wasn't sure if the boy was simple or just shy.

"Nice to meet you, Henry. My name is Sergeant Bowen, but you can call me Kaci if you like. I'm with the RCMP. I suppose you know why I'm here?"

"You came to look after Mr Tull," Henry said, shuffling his feet and peering around her trying to get a look inside the room.

"Yes. That's right," she replied.

Henry looked directly at her and asked again, "Is he really dead?"

"Yes. He's dead."

Henry nodded his head as he processed the information. He had a serious look on his face, but didn't seem upset. Sergeant Bowen wasn't overly surprised by this. Young people in farm country were raised knowing death was as natural as birth and were often able to handle it better than some adults she knew.

"Do you know what happened to him?" the boy asked.

"Not yet, but I'm sure we'll figure it out. And you might be able to help."

"How? I just found him, that's all," Henry said.

"Did you happen to hear or see anything unusual this morning?"

Henry considered her question for a moment.

She continued, "If I understand it right, you went to get him for breakfast."

Henry nodded again. "Gramma Carol asked me to let him know it was ready. That was one of my usual morning jobs."

"Do you have other jobs you do in the morning?" she asked.

"I do my math homework first thing before breakfast. Gramma Carol says my brain is sharpest then."

Sergeant Bowen pulled out her notepad and pencil. "Do you mind if I take a few notes?"

"No, ma'am. I mean, that would be fine," Henry answered.

"My mind isn't as good at remembering as it used to be," she joked. "When was the last time you saw Mr Tull, other than this morning?"

"Last night, before bed."

"And where did you see him?"

"In there," Henry said, pointing to the writing room. "I took him his evening tonic."

"Tonic?"

Henry smiled. "That's what Gramma Carol calls it. It's a gross thing he likes to drink before bed. I wouldn't drink it if you paid me."

"Do you know what's in this tonic?"

"I think there's brandy, but you have to ask Gramma Carol."

"And you usually bring it to Mr Tull before bed?" Sergeant Bowen asked.

"No. Gramma Carol does. I'm usually in bed before ten and that's when Mr Tull has it. At ten p.m. sharp, but I was up late looking at the stars, so I said I could take it to him."

Sergeant Bowen carefully noted the time.

"You said ten p.m. sharp. So, I gather Mr Tull is strict about schedules?"

"Yes ma'am. He's strict—I mean, he *was* strict—about a lot of things."

"What sorts of things?"

"When I didn't bring his afternoon coffee at two p.m., he would yell 'Discipline is the only thing that stops us from sliding back to the stone age.'"

Sergeant Bowen smiled. Her inspector had said something similar that very morning.

"And last night when you brought him his tonic, were you on time?" she continued.

"Yes, ma'am."

"And you didn't wait to see if he drank his tonic?"

"No, ma'am, I didn't. Mr Tull told me to leave him alone."

A low growl sounded from Henry's stomach.

Sergeant Bowen closed her notebook. "I won't keep you and your stomach much longer. Was there anything at all that you can think of that was…different this morning?"

Henry smiled. "I got Gramma Carol real good with a math joke. I told her I like pi."

"Good one," Sergeant Bowen said, pretending she got the joke. "Okay, anything else you remember from last night or this morning?"

"No, ma'am. Not that I can think of right now."

"Thank you, Henry. You've been very helpful. Would you get your Gramma Carol for me?"

"Sure," Henry said, then disappeared out of sight.

Sergeant Bowen walked back into the writing room and looked out through the window to see if there was any sign of the coroner or forensics team. Behind her, someone cleared their throat and Sergeant Bowen turned and saw the woman who had let her into the house earlier…Mrs Cameron.

Sergeant Bowen studied her for a moment. Mrs Cameron was old, mid-eighties the sergeant guessed, around one-hundred-and-seventy centimetres with a weight of seventy kilograms. Mrs Cameron dressed the part of a housekeeper with a loose-fitting dress that came down to her ankles, a white apron and comfortable black running shoes. Her white hair was unevenly cut short and parted on the left side. She had probably cut it herself.

"You wanted to see me?"

"Mrs Cameron, do you know if Mr Tull had any medical issues?"

"All I know is he took pills every night with his tonic. I'm not sure what they were for since he bragged about how healthy he was. He went running every morning at dawn, at least in the summer months. In the winter he'd bundle up and head out for a brisk walk." She folded her arms. "He had the nerve to say that if Mr Pritchard had taken better care of himself, he wouldn't have dropped dead like he did."

"Mr Pritchard?" Sergeant Bowen asked.

"That was the previous writer-in-residence at Hoodoo House," Mrs Cameron replied.

"And exactly what did Mr Pritchard die of?" Sergeant Bowen asked.

Mrs Cameron scowled. "Old age."

Sergeant Bowen looked down at her notes. "Henry said that you prepare Mr Tull's evening tonic. What precisely does it contain?"

"It's *kumis*, a drink made from fermented mare's milk. He claimed it was the fountain of youth. He makes it himself. I just serve it up to him with a shot of brandy. I told him to forget the yogourty glop and stick to the brandy. It would probably do the same thing for him."

Sergeant Bowen made a note, then pushed ahead. "And how long have you known Mr Tull?"

Mrs Cameron paused. "A little over fifteen years, I guess. He started out as Mr Pritchard's editor before taking over the position of writer-in-residence."

"Is that normal? An editor becoming a writer?"

"Sometimes. And sometimes it happens the other way around."

Bowen turned the page on her notepad. "What exactly does a writer-in-residence do?"

"Here, the writer-in-residence is a fully supported position. They get a place to stay, meals, a monthly stipend and a place far away from distraction to create whatever they want."

"And who pays for all of this?"

"The Heart's Shadow Foundation," Mrs Cameron said, "and before you ask, they get their money from the proceeds of Marjorie Ellis' *The Heart's Shadow* book series."

Sergeant Bowen frowned. "*The Heart's Shadow*, huh? I've never heard of it. It must be a profitable book series to support all this."

"It is. You obviously aren't from around here, are you?" Mrs Cameron said.

"Brandon, Manitoba, actually. I transferred here two months ago."

Sergeant Bowen glanced around the writing room before continuing, "Running this place must cost a lot of money. These writers, they must be good." She hoped to placate her.

"Mr Pritchard was," Mrs Cameron sharply replied.

"And Mr Tull?"

"He was…competent."

Mrs Cameron started to fuss with something in her apron pocket. "May I?" she asked as she entered the room and walked towards the desk, pulling out a cleaning rag.

"Mrs Cameron, please don't touch anything," the sergeant said, stepping between her and the desk.

"Look, I've already been in here once today. I'll just clean up the vomit."

"Mrs Cameron, I'm afraid I can't let you touch it."

"But the desk is a valuable piece of furniture. The stomach acid could damage it!"

"It might also hold evidence as to what happened here."

"But…that's the very desk Marjorie Ellis wrote *The Ragtag Crew* at…"

Sergeant Bowen took her by the arm. "Mrs Cameron, what would help me most is if you would leave everything just as it is until forensics has been through."

The housekeeper took one more glance at the desk and shook her head. "Fine," she said then marched out of the room.

* * * *

Forensics arrived and inspected the body. They removed the hard evidence, including the *kumis* mug, the pill bottle and a large sample of the vomit from the desk. The coroner examined Tull's body then took it away for further inspection. The room almost looked like nothing had happened, except for the yellow police tape which blocked the entrance to the writing room.

Sergeant Bowen went outside onto the veranda, took out a pack of cigarettes and extracted a smoke. As she lit it up, she looked out at the prairie before her. It was harvest-time. There was a combination of yellows, golds, clay browns and endless blue sky. The world was filled with the sound of buzzing insects. It had life and colour, unlike the house which was in desperate need of repairs and a fresh coat of paint. A twenty-foot-tall narrow stack of fake reddish-brown rocks with a stone plate on top stood on guard near the entrance of the house. It looked like it was made of coloured concrete and chicken wire. To the side of it was a sign that read "The Spirit of the Hoodoo".

An insult to the hoodoos, if you ask me.

This place gave her the creeps. It would give the Bates house from *Psycho* a run for its money.

Bowen took a final drag on her cigarette, flicked the stub onto the ground then crushed it with her heel.

If I had to live in this house, I might consider taking my own life, she mused, then walked back to her car and drove away.

* * * *

For a long time after the police had left, Henry sat on the swinging bench on the south porch. There was a freedom in swinging. The gentle motion helped to calm him. And there was always a gentle breeze blowing over the hill to the west. Whenever he needed peace and quiet when the weather was pleasant, this was where he went.

He rifled through the comic books that he'd brought with him and pulled out one from the series *Momrath and The Slithe*. The Slithe was his favourite superhero. He was powerful, even if he was a slim guy in a shiny skin-tight black costume. Few dared to bother him, but if they did, The Slithe could deal with them. And The Slithe believed in justice.

Henry was reading the current issue for the fourth time when he heard the deep rumble of a motorcycle engine. A familiar bike made its way up the long drive from the concession road. It moved slowly towards the house, then the driver killed the engine so the only noise was the crunching of rubber tires on gravel. As the bike came to a halt, the rider dropped the kickstand and dismounted. He took off his helmet and hung it from the handlebars. Henry recognized the man. He was one of Mr Tull's visitors. The man looked fit and not that old, not like Mr Tull. Not even as old as Mr Yamada, the editor.

"Hey kid."

"Hey."

The biker started to walk towards the house.

"Mr Tull's not there," Henry said. "He's dead."

For the first time, Henry noticed how much the rider looked like The Slithe. He wore heavy leather clothes, but he doubted the biker's motorcycle was made of pure diamond like The Slithe's was.

There was a long silence before the rider asked, "You okay?"

"I guess," Henry said. "I'd never seen a dead body before."

"Sorry you had to see that."

The rider looked at the window at the front of the house — the window which belonged to the writer's office. He stared at it for a long time, while he chewed on his lower lip.

"Look, kid, I left something here with Mr Tull. I was hoping to pick it up today. I think it's in his office. Mind if I go in and check?"

Henry was about to answer when the front door of the house swung open. Gramma Carol came striding out onto the porch. She had her rolling pin in her hand.

"I don't know what you're doing, but you've got no business here. Now get off this property before I call the cops."

Henry smiled. Gramma Carol was a lot like a superhero. She always used reason before she resorted to using a weapon, in this case her rolling pin.

The man shrugged and headed back to his bike. He got on slowly. Henry grinned.

He doesn't want Gramma Carol to see that she won.

But Henry also suspected that he didn't want to be on the receiving end of that piece of smooth rounded maple. The man started up his bike and motored back down the drive.

"What did he want?" she asked Henry.

"He said he forgot something here."

"His decency, I'll bet."

She shook her head and returned into the house.

Henry thought that Gramma Carol deserved to have her own comic book. The villains wouldn't have a chance.

Chapter One

Charlie's stomach grumbled. He was hungry and though Declan had picked him up a latte, he hadn't brought him a pastry. When Charlie went to the café he always bought treats, but Declan had made it a personal rule never to buy them. Whenever Charlie came upstairs with sweets, Declan acted like a five-year-old who was told that he had to eat Brussels sprouts. He'd say that he was afraid they'd go right to his waist. Charlie found his mind drifting above Declan's waist to his beautifully sculpted abs. It would take a lot of pastries to undo that physique.

Charlie shook his head and made his way to Declan's office. "I just have to pop out for a sec. Be right back."

"Don't go bringing cookies into this place," Declan said without looking up. Charlie smiled.

On his way down to the café, he thought about the decision he'd recently made regarding his relationship with Declan. He was convinced he'd made the right choice. *I'm here to keep things running efficiently – and that's it. It wouldn't make sense to mix business with pleasure.* But a little voice in the back of his head kept asking, *How are you going to feel if Declan finds someone else?* Charlie knew how sick he'd felt when Declan had fallen for that cop Luke while working on the Ian Mann case a few months ago. Sure, that hadn't worked out, but if Charlie didn't make a move soon…

Charlie exited onto the street. Loud voices were coming from the café. The words were muffled. He couldn't make out their meaning, but the intention was clear. Someone was giving the owner Gwen a hard time. Charlie rushed through the door and saw that Gwen was going head-to-head with a very large cop who was waving a parking ticket in her face.

"So you're telling me you can't fix this for me?" she hollered, poking the cop in the shoulder. "I've parked there ever since I opened this place and no one's complained about it before!"

"I'm just saying the cop that issued this ticket was right," he yelled back. "They changed the rules and now you have to pay for street parking from nine a.m. to four p.m."

Charlie recognized the voice.

"Good morning, Sergeant Hunt," he said. The cop was Gwen's husband…and Declan's father.

"Charlie, maybe you can talk some sense into this woman," he said before storming out of the café.

"What was all that about?" Charlie asked.

"What good is being married to a cop if he won't fix a traffic ticket for you?"

She glanced out of the window and yelled, "Don't you dare put it back on my windshield!"

"Men," she muttered before heading back around

the counter. She shook her head and smiled at Charlie. "Now, what can I get you?"

A man of my own that I can yell at? Charlie thought.

"A scone, please," he answered. "Better make it two."

Gwen raised her eyebrows.

"Don't worry. They're both for me."

"Good. I don't want to get yelled at by two Hunts in one day," she said, packing up the pastries.

Charlie shot her a crooked smile then headed back up to the office, pastries in hand. Declan had said not to come back with cookies but he'd said nothing about scones.

Charlie took a swig of his latte and munched on one of his scones before heading into Declan's office. Declan sat deep in thought staring at a picture in a silver frame which he held in his hand. Charlie paused, then knocked on the door jamb.

"I had a call from Mr Attwal this morning."

Declan set down the frame and looked blankly at Charlie. "Sorry. What did you say?"

"Mr Attwal. He has our monthly accounting statements ready. It's good news. We're in the black."

"Good to know," he said.

Charlie pointed to the framed portrait. "That's a good-looking young man. Is he a relative of yours?"

Declan shook his head. "No. Just someone from a long time ago."

Charlie considered offering Declan one of the scones as comfort food, but knew better. Then he remembered. "Oh, by any chance did you receive an email from the Alberta LGBTQ+ Business Association? Actually, did you receive six emails from them over the last few days?"

"Who the hell are they?"

"Well, if I were to take a wild shot at it, I'd guess that they're an association of LGBTQ+ business owners."

Declan smirked. "You'll make a great detective someday."

"Thank you. Anyway, I had a call from them this morning. They sounded a little stressed. It seems that they give out an annual 'local hero' award. A pretty big deal, from what I've read online. Apparently they chose you as this year's recipient."

"Oh…?"

"And they haven't heard back from you. They weren't sure if you were even still alive given the lack of communication."

"Well, I've been busy," he said.

"They've been a bit busy as well. Seems that you weren't their first choice. That was City Councillor Frasniak."

Declan scowled. "Why's that name ring a bell?"

"He was just charged with six counts of misappropriation of city funds and two counts of bribery."

"Oooo," Declan said. "There's a hero for you."

"But you've always been their second choice. It was a close race."

"I guess Frasniak was offering better bribes." Declan smiled.

"Funny."

"So when's the award being given out?"

"Friday night," Charlie replied.

"This Friday?"

"Yeah. But I'm sure if they could have arranged to have Councillor Frasniak arrested sooner, they would have been able to give you more notice. Think of it this way—it would be such great publicity for the firm…"

Declan crossed his arms.

Charlie continued. "And you'd be helping them out, something that you're known for in the community, which is *why* they want to give you the award."

Declan sighed. "Okay. Call them back and tell them I'd be honoured to accept it."

As Charlie turned to leave Declan asked, "So, do they just mail the award-thing out?"

Charlie turned back and smiled. "Oh, right. I meant to tell you…it's a full ceremony. The award is presented at the Lambda Ball at the Palliser Hotel. It's the biggest event of their season. Every queen in Alberta will be there."

"Oh."

"And it's black tie. Is it safe to assume that we'll be needing to rent you one for the evening?"

Declan raised his eyebrows. "No. As a matter of fact, I actually have my own."

Charlie pictured Declan in a tux and his heart began to race. "By the way… It's customary for the honouree to bring a date for the evening…"

Declan stared Charlie in the eyes for a moment. "Well, I guess I'll be going stag then."

"Oh." Charlie's voice quavered.

"Unless…you'd like to be my date?"

"Really?" Charlie squeaked.

Declan laughed. "Why not? I can't think of a better person to take to the ball."

"Thank you. I'd…I'll need to rent something. Do you mind if I take the rest of the morning off?"

"No problem. And charge it to the company."

As Charlie turned to leave, Declan called out, "Stop."

He beckoned Charlie with his finger. When Charlie got to Declan's desk, his boss motioned for him to come closer. Charlie's heart pounded. When he stood an arm's length away, Declan reached up and plucked a large flake of pastry off of Charlie's shirt, then popped it into his own mouth and sighed.

"Gwen's pastries…so good, and so evil," was all he said.

Charlie sailed back to the outer office and noticed a flashing light on the phone. He picked up the receiver, pressed a button on the phone and listened to the message. It was from someone named Sinclair Yamada who wanted to discuss a potential case with Declan. Charlie tried calling back, but it went straight to voicemail. He left a message, then quickly placed a call to the gay business association to tell them that Declan would be honoured to accept their award. Charlie added that Declan would be accompanied by his partner. He purposely failed to elaborate on the term. Charlie grinned as he headed out of the door.

Time to go and rent my tuxedo and glass slippers for the ball.

* * * *

Declan sat at his desk and stared out through the window. He'd invited Charlie to a ball. Declan had to admit that the thought of taking Charlie somewhere on a date had been crossing his mind more and more. The look on his face when he'd asked him…he was certain he'd seen tears.

But he had promised Charlie that their relationship would be business-only, and he had promised himself that he'd respect Charlie's wishes. And in spite of how much Declan hated a public fuss, he would go along with attending the awards ceremony for the sake of the business.

He looked back at the framed portrait of the teen. "What do you think? Do I really deserve this?"

Chapter Two

One of the perks that came along with being an award winner was the use of a rented limousine. The driver picked Declan up at the office, then drove the short distance to where Charlie was living.

Declan rang the doorbell for the second-floor unit of the modest, neatly-kept two-storey detached house. Carrie, Charlie's roommate, answered. Declan recognized her the moment she opened the door even though they had only met once before. Carrie looked Declan up and down, then smiled.

"Looking good," she said, nodding her head. "Come on in. Charlie's still getting ready."

She led him up the stairs and into the living room.

"I don't know what's keeping him. He never takes this long to get ready. Can I get you a drink?"

"Thank you." Declan took a seat on the couch. The room was filled with over-stuffed furniture that was far from new. The couch was covered with a hand-crocheted afghan, and the rest of the furniture had a sense of second-hand-chic. It was a comfortable home.

Carrie came back in with a couple of glasses of wine. She gave Declan one then took the chair opposite him.

"So…Declan. That's Irish isn't it?"

"Yes. My mother's family was Irish. I was named after her father."

"It's a beautiful name."

"Apparently it means 'man of prayer', although my father claims I don't have one. A prayer, that is."

Carrie smiled.

"I hope the same won't be said about Charlie. As I recall, the last time you picked him up here, you brought him back in rougher shape than he left."

Declan remembered the night he had driven Charlie back home from Airdrie after his second undercover mission.

"I can promise you that tonight will be a party compared to that."

Declan realized that they were no longer alone. He looked towards the hallway, and there was Charlie, perfectly handsome in his tuxedo, every hair on his head tamed into place. He was the vision of an angel. Declan had to remember to breathe.

Carrie turned and let out a near-silent "Oh my God."

"I hope I didn't keep you," Charlie said.

"No. Not at all." Declan couldn't take his eyes off of him.

"Now, before you two head out, I have to get a picture," Carrie said, pulling out her cell phone.

"Carrie," Charlie whined.

"I'm not going to miss getting a picture of you looking this fine. The next time might not be 'til your funeral."

"Come on," Declan said. "Where would you like us?"

"Over there," Carrie said, pointing to a wall covered in large framed photos.

Declan led Charlie over to the wall, and pulled him near, putting his arm around his waist. They let Carrie take several shots before Declan said, "We should probably be heading out."

As Charlie passed Carrie, Declan heard her whisper, "So sweet. Just like going to prom."

"Bitch," Charlie whispered.

"That's *jealous* bitch to you," she whispered back.

* * * *

The limo pulled up under the ornate marquee of the Fairmont Palliser Hotel. The doorman instantly appeared and opened the door of the car. Charlie slipped out first, hoping that maybe a photographer would be there to notice them. Declan exited the car with less haste. As he did, an older man burst through the hotel doors and scurried down the steps. He looked like a rat escaping a cat. His nose was aquiline with a hooked tip. On his upper lip he sported a wispy, unshaped moustache which nicely complemented what little hair he had on the top of his head. His teeth were somewhat crooked and bucked.

"Mr Hunt," he wheezed out. "I'm so glad you're here."

Charlie wondered if they were late. He checked his watch and they were only a few minutes behind schedule.

As the man caught his breath he said, "I'm Roger Honeyfield, Chair of the ALGBTQ+BA. I'm your host for this evening."

Honeyfield reached out his hand towards Declan,

who shook it firmly. Honeyfield then turned to Charlie. "And you are?"

"Charlie Watts. I'm with him," he said, pointing to Declan.

"Charles. So nice to meet you."

"It's Charlie—"

Honeyfield cut him off abruptly, turning back to Declan. "I'm sorry I wasn't here waiting for you when you arrived," he said as he leaned in towards the open car door, "but your driver didn't give me the requisite notice…like he said he would."

"I did call you in time. Maybe if you'd had your phone turned on…" the driver answered in a sarcastic tone.

"That'll be enough from you, Douglas," Honeyfield snapped, slamming the car door as he did.

Honeyfield sighed. "To think I used to date him." He shook his head and sighed again. Charlie looked at Declan, stifling a smile.

"If you'll please follow me," Honeyfield said as he scurried back up the stairs ahead of them.

When they arrived at the entrance to the event's venue—the Crystal Ballroom—Honeyfield pulled the two aside and confessed in a hushed tone, "We have uncovered a little…challenge that I would prefer not to get out. Many of our…members"—he rotated his head to glower at the other guests in the room—"would love to get wind of this. They'd do anything to see me fail."

He leaned in closer. "I was the one who, unfortunately, nominated Frasniak. How was I to know he was a crooked politician, or at least a politician who was inept enough to get caught? They've had their knives out for me ever since. And now this!" He paused for a moment.

"If you don't mind me asking, Roger, what is *this*?" Declan asked, in a hushed tone. Charlie was enjoying himself.

Honeyfield continued, "The award, of course. The medallion we're presenting to you. It's been inscribed with that moron Frasniak's name, not yours." He grabbed Declan by the sleeve of his jacket. "If they ever find out, I'm done for."

Declan smiled and took Honeyfield's hand. "Roger, don't worry. My job is to keep secrets. I'll make sure no one finds out."

"Oh, thank you. Thank you so much," he said as he spun on his heels and entered the ballroom.

"Really? 'My job is to keep secrets'?" Charlie whispered to Declan with a grin.

Declan shrugged his shoulders.

"Mr Hunt, Charles, would you follow me, please?" Honeyfield called out.

"Uh…it's Charlie!" Charlie corrected again.

Declan looked at him and smirked. He offered Charlie his arm and the two of them entered the ballroom.

The room was decorated in soft blues and golds and illuminated by thirteen large crystal chandeliers. Charlie had read that it could hold over three hundred guests. He estimated that there were only about a hundred there tonight.

"I'm so pleased to see a big crowd," Honeyfield crowed. "Ticket sales really took off when we announced you as the recipient of this year's Vriend Medal."

When they walked into the room, all eyes turned towards them…hungry eyes of gay men scoping out the handsome detective and… Their gazes said it—*Who is that slim young man with him?*

"The plan for the evening," Honeyfield said as he paraded them around the room, "is drinks and canapés, followed by introductions and the presentation of the Vriend Medal. Then your speech, of course, before we move on to…well, more drinks and food and dancing! Now, I'll leave you to mingle with the guests."

Before Declan or Charlie could say anything, Honeyfield had spun around and headed towards the nearest drink-toting waiter.

Declan had a concerned look on his face. "A speech? I didn't know anything about a speech? Did you know anything about a speech?"

"No," Charlie replied. "No one said anything at all about you making a speech. But I wouldn't worry about it. Just say something like, 'Thanks, this really means a lot to me. It justifies my existence', that sort of thing. From the looks of it, these people are just happy to throw back a bunch of drinks and stare at a hot award-winning detective."

Declan stared at Charlie.

"Oh, come on," Charlie said, "You do know how great you look in that tux, don't you? It fits you like it was painted on."

"Look," Declan said as he grabbed Charlie by the shoulders and pulled him closer. "I can face a killer with a gun pressed against my head, or take a few good kicks to the gut, but speaking in public…it really isn't my thing."

It was at that moment Honeyfield mounted the steps to the podium, tapped the microphone and started to talk. Declan looked towards the door like he was going to make a run for it. Charlie reached over to an older gentleman and grabbed his drink which had just been delivered by a waiter. "I need this. Emergency," Charlie said.

"Drink this. Now!" Charlie handed the glass to Declan. The detective did as he was instructed.

Charlie continued, "Okay, when the time comes, you are going to walk up to that podium. When you climb those three steps, you are going to flex those ass muscles of yours. I don't care if that tux is made of painter's canvas, people will notice. They're going to give you that medal, or whatever it is, and you will turn to the audience and smile. Just say 'Thank you. You have no idea what this means to me.' At that point everyone here will be thinking of nothing else but how gorgeous you are."

In the background Honeyfield's speech droned on. He spoke of the man that the medal was named for—Delwin Vriend—and how his fight for equal rights should be a lesson to everyone there. He continued to deliver the speech with a complete lack of passion, which didn't surprise Charlie in the least.

"… And as you all know, this year's recipient of the Vriend Medal, for his support of the LGBTQ+ community, is Declan Hunt, a man who has dedicated his career to fighting for individuals who have been forgotten by the public servants who have been entrusted with that…sacred task."

Charlie managed to get one more drink into Declan before the moment came. Honeyfield crowed, "And now, please welcome to the stage, this year's winner of the Vriend Medal, Declan Hunt."

The detective walked with confidence, then climbed, flexing with every stair. Honeyfield placed a beautiful silver medallion suspended on a rainbow-coloured ribbon around Declan's neck. The detective turned and smiled. A hundred hearts fluttered. Declan looked around the room, then locked eyes with Charlie.

Declan took a deep breath and began. "The thought of speaking in public terrifies me, but my assistant, Charlie Watts, told me simply to say, 'Thank you. You have no idea how much this means to me.'"

Declan held the medal and looked at it.

"I didn't understand how much this would mean until Roger put it around my neck. Looking at it now, I realize why I do what I do." Declan cleared his throat. "You see…one of the first cases I worked on as a police constable was the disappearance of a young boy. His name was" — he swallowed again — "Freddy Whitcher. Two days ago would have been his birthday. He was only thirteen back then and, when his father found out that he was gay, he beat him. He beat him every night for two weeks until Freddy had finally had enough. So he ran away from home and away from his family who were supposed to love and protect him. He wound up living on the streets."

There was a catch in Declan's voice. Charlie stepped closer to the stage, in front of the podium and willed him to keep going.

Declan took a sip of water and continued, "Can you imagine what it was like for that thirteen-year-old kid trying to survive alone on the streets of Calgary? In the winter? Can you imagine the things he had to do just to stay alive?"

The room was silent. No one moved. All eyes were focused on Declan.

"I was the cop who found Freddy, or what was left of him. No one knew whether he just got too close to the fire trying to stay warm or… It was at that moment that I knew that I was going to dedicate my life to helping people like Freddy or anyone in our community who needs help fighting against prejudice, discrimination and hatred, especially from those who are supposed to be out there protecting them. I discovered I couldn't do that fully as a member of the Calgary Police Service so I had to go out on my own. And if I can succeed, maybe, just maybe, Freddy can forgive me for not finding him in time. So I accept this award in honour of him. Thank you."

Declan stepped down from the podium, and the room erupted into applause. As he walked towards Charlie, people shook Declan's hand. Others hugged him after wiping away their tears. From behind him Charlie heard, "How could you not fall in love with that man?"

Charlie made his way towards Declan and put his arms around him.

"Freddy's the boy in the picture on your desk, isn't he?" Charlie asked.

"Yeah." Declan just kept holding on to Charlie, and Charlie didn't mind.

The moment was broken as a live band began to play an upbeat song and people started to dance. Charlie pulled himself back from Declan and started gyrating and stomping his feet to the beat, smiling and never taking his eyes off Declan.

"What are you doing?" Declan asked.

"Dancing," Charlie called out. "Carrie and I go out every weekend. You should try it!" Charlie spun around, almost taking out Roger, who was zeroing in on Declan.

"Mr Hunt, would you care to dance?" Honeyfield said, awkwardly moving his arms and swaying his shoulders.

"I'm afraid Mr Hunt has promised me the first dance," Charlie said, then took Declan by the hand and moved onto the dance floor.

Declan mouthed the words 'thank you' as he followed.

Over the next thirty minutes, whenever Charlie saw Honeyfield approach, he would start to flail his arms and take leaping strides, spinning around Declan, building a shield of limbs to shelter the handsome detective from the approaching enemy. Declan just laughed.

There was a brief lull in the music. Charlie and Declan were both panting from the exertion of dancing. When the band began to play again, it was a slow dance. Charlie moved to leave the dance floor when he felt a hand in his. Charlie turned and saw Declan standing there, no smile on his face, just a look of...something.

"Now it's my turn to ask you to dance."

Charlie allowed himself to be drawn in close. He could feel Declan's muscular chest against his slim torso. One of Declan's hands pressed against the small of his back, holding Charlie close to his body. Charlie hesitantly put his arm around Declan's back and held tight. He'd never slow-danced with a man before. Charlie nuzzled his face into Declan's neck as they swayed across the dance floor to a song that Charlie hoped would never end.

Chapter Three

The evening came to a close at around eleven o'clock. As they made their way out of the ballroom and down the stairs towards the front door of the hotel, Charlie heard footsteps quickly approaching from behind. He turned, expecting he'd have to fend off Roger Honeyfield. Instead it was an attractive Asian man in a nicely tailored charcoal-grey suit. He looked to be in his mid-thirties. He wore horn-rimmed glasses and had a strong square jaw. Charlie thought he looked like a manga comic book version of Clark Kent.

"Mr Hunt. May I have a word with you?" he asked as he caught up with them at the front door.

"Sure," Declan replied.

"This may take a while. Can I buy the two of you a drink?"

"Sure," Declan answered, like it was the only word he had left in his vocabulary. It was clear he was tired and that the stress of the event had taken a toll on him. Charlie suspected that, if the man who had approached them hadn't been so attractive, they would be heading out of the door instead of having drinks with him.

"By the way," Charlie said, extending his hand, "I'm Charlie Watts."

"Like the drummer! Nice to meet you, Charlie," he said without offering his name back.

The man led them to the lobby bar. As they wound their way to a table in the far corner, Charlie whispered to Declan, "What's this guy want to say to you that he couldn't have said at the party?"

Declan shrugged. "I guess we're going to find out."

"I hope this is comfortable enough for you," the man said as they sat. "Now, I was watching the two of you and I don't think you've had anything to eat all night. Shall we order some food?"

Charlie had already begun to look at the menu. "That would be great. Thanks."

The man motioned the waiter over. Once their order was taken and the waiter had departed, the man looked around, then turned back to face them. "Now, I should introduce myself. My name is Sinclair Yamada."

Charlie recognized the name. "You called earlier this week."

"Yes, and I received your return message. Thanks for getting back to me." He turned to Declan. "I already had my ticket for the event tonight, so when I heard that you would be here, I thought I might just as well approach you in person. I hope you don't mind."

"No problem," Declan said.

Charlie was concerned. Declan seemed to be just a shell of his usual self. He wished this Yamada guy would just get to the point so Charlie could get Declan home. Charlie decided he would have to take charge.

"If I remember right," Charlie said, "you work for Mount Temple Press."

"Yes. Are you familiar with the company?"

Declan's face remained blank.

"They're an important Canadian publisher," Charlie explained.

"Ah," Declan grunted.

Charlie turned back to Mr Yamada. "So, how exactly can we help you?"

"Mount Temple Press operates a charitable trust. Through it we provide a retreat at Hoodoo House near Rosebud with full support services, as well as a stipend to worthy writers who generate novels for the publisher."

"*Generate* novels?" Declan echoed. "That's an odd way to put it."

Mr Yamada's face flushed. "I'll have you know that we give them a safe creative space and promise them all the support that they need on their road to publication."

Charlie stammered "I think…what Declan meant to say was—"

"Forgive me," Yamada interrupted. "I didn't mean to sound defensive, it's just that we've been under a great deal of stress lately. You see, last week Malcolm Tull, our latest writer-in-residence, was found dead at Hoodoo House."

"So, not such a safe creative space after all," Declan said.

"The coroner is still looking into it, but apparently Mr Tull had more than the usual amount of his medication in his system."

"Suicide?" Charlie asked.

Mr Yamada leaned in. "According to the coroner, there was also some bruising on his neck. They're treating the death as suspicious."

Declan shrugged. "That sounds like something the police should deal with."

"His death, yes, but there's something else I need your help with," Mr Yamada said. "Mr Tull's computer is missing and it's essential that I get it back. The only known copy of his latest manuscript is on it."

Yamada stopped suddenly as the waiter appeared, placing two scotches, an imported beer and a fourteen-dollar basket of salted fries on the table. Mr Yamada waited until the server had departed before knocking back his scotch and asking, "So can you help me?"

Declan swirled the scotch in his glass. "A missing computer? That's still a job for the cops."

"That is precisely what I am trying to avoid," Yamada whispered.

"What are you trying to avoid?" Charlie asked.

"The police finding the computer first."

Declan cocked his head. "Go on."

"Malcolm Tull could be very charismatic when he wanted to be," Mr Yamada said as he signalled the waiter.

"Would you care for another, sir?" the waiter asked.

"Make it a double," he said, tapping his fingers on the table.

He turned to Declan and Charlie. "Malcolm and I, we…had sex. Just once! I swear it. It was highly inappropriate given our relationship."

"And your relationship was?" Declan asked.

"I was unlucky enough to be his editor."

"Why do you say unlucky?" Declan asked.

"Malcolm Tull was a nasty son of a bitch to most people. He was self-centred, verging on narcissistic, never admitted to being wrong and he treated all others as inferiors. I don't know anyone who got along with him."

"Yet you still chose to sleep with him," Declan said.

"Have you never done anything, Mr Hunt, that you

have regretted?"

"Point taken," Declan said, nodding.

Charlie munched on the French fries and watched the show.

"Yet, in spite of his vast personality flaws," Yamada continued, "there was something—an attraction. I mean, he was a good-looking man. And fit. And he was *very* good at sex."

"And what part of that makes you think I can help you?" Declan asked. "I can't turn back time and make your romp with him disappear."

"No. But I'm hoping you can find his computer that also contains the video of the encounter."

"Oh shit." The words slipped out of Charlie's mouth before he could stop them.

"Oh shit indeed," Yamada said. "Needless to say, I need to ensure nobody else gets their hands on that computer."

"You let him record the encounter?" Declan asked.

"No, I most certainly did not. I didn't find out about it until recently when he sent me an email with screen captures of the video's kinkier moments. He informed me that it would remain hidden if I—"

"He was blackmailing you?" Charlie interrupted.

"What did he want?" Declan asked.

"He told me that my employer would not see the video if I pushed through his latest novel as written. '*Verbatim ac litteratim*' as he put it, the arrogant shit."

"Word for word and letter for letter," Charlie recited.

"Correct," Yamada said, nodding towards Charlie.

Declan continued, "Now, I assume that just printing what the writer gives you, without editing the content, is out of the ordinary."

"More than that—it isn't done! And the manuscript

has to be approved by the publisher. Those are the rules. I couldn't do it if I wanted to. You see, the novel he was proposing was...not on brand."

"I assume you told him that," Declan said.

"I most certainly did. And from what he intimated about the contents of the book, I told him it was definitely not suitable for Mount Temple Press and would never be approved by the publisher."

"And how did he react?"

"He just laughed and said 'Find a way, bright boy.'"

"And he told you he kept the video on his computer?" Declan asked.

"When I last saw him, he said the files were on his computer, which was someplace safe."

"And now both the computer and Mr Tull are gone," Declan pondered aloud.

"I'm not sure if it's stolen or hidden, but wherever it is, it is essential that I get that computer back with the manuscript...and any video. My reputation and career are at stake."

The waiter brought Mr Yamada's double scotch to the table. Before the server could leave, Mr Yamada swigged the entire drink back in one swallow, then indicated the waiter should bring the bill.

"So will you take the case? After all, gay sex and blackmail seem right up your alley. And I need complete discretion."

Declan nodded. "Let us do a bit of checking first, but sure, we're interested. We'll be in touch with you on Monday."

As Charlie took down Sinclair's contact information, the waiter approached Declan carrying a silver platter on which lay a perfect red rose. "A gift from a gentleman, sir."

Declan looked at Charlie.

"It wasn't me," Charlie said. *I wish it was.*

Sinclair smiled. "It seems that you have an admirer."

Declan looked around to see if he was being watched, but aside from the waiter, they were the only ones remaining in the bar. There was, however, a business card tucked under the rose. It was Roger Honeyfield's.

* * * *

The limo ride home was quiet. Declan stared out of the window. Charlie assumed he was thinking about their new client. As the car pulled up to Charlie's place, he turned to Declan and said, "Well, that was an interesting night. Thanks for taking me as your date. And we got a new case."

He reached for the door handle but Declan stopped him. "Wait. I want you to know that I couldn't have made it through the ceremony tonight without you."

"Oh, it was nothing, really. It's all part of the job," Charlie said.

"No. It was more than that. If it wasn't for you, I would have made a run for it before the evening got started."

Charlie smiled. "Thanks."

"And you surprised me," Declan said. "You're not a bad dancer."

"Neither are you."

Declan picked up the rose from the seat beside him and handed it to Charlie. "I want you to have this," he said, staring into Charlie's eyes, a gentle smile on his face.

Charlie took the rose then leaned in, intending to give Declan a gentle kiss on the lips, but once he'd started he found himself unable to pull away. A mechanical whir came out of nowhere. The screen which separated the driver from the passenger compartment was rising to give them privacy.

Charlie dropped the rose on the floor and launched himself at Declan, pinning him into the far corner of the bench seat, holding him by the wrists. Charlie kissed him more deeply, tasting the smokiness of the scotch that lingered in Declan's mouth.

Charlie drew his knees up until he was straddling Declan.

Declan gently pushed Charlie back and looked him in the eyes. "If we do this, there's no going back."

"I don't care," Charlie replied then moved in again.

Declan began to kiss Charlie, then stopped and pushed Charlie to the other side of the seat. "I'm sorry. I can't. I don't want to screw this up. We had an amazing time tonight, but we've both had a lot to drink, and I'm not thinking clearly. You're just swept up in the moment."

Charlie gritted his teeth. *In the moment? It's been a whole evening. It's been months. You started this!*

"What's wrong with you? I thought this was what you wanted," Charlie said.

"I do but…I've been thinking a lot about this and I just can't. Not tonight. Not this way."

"Fine!"

Charlie straightened himself up, opened the car door and said, "I guess I'll see you at work on Monday. It's all business from now on."

As Charlie got out of the limo, Declan held the flower out to him and said, "Charlie, I'm sorry."

"You can keep your fucking rose," Charlie said, then slammed the car door and ran up the walk and into the house.

Chapter Four

All of the next day, Declan was feeling uneasy. His life had always been in a state of flux, but his personal life was getting...complicated, in ways that he didn't want to admit to Charlie. Declan had trouble focusing and even abandoned his Saturday work-out. By the time he finished dinner, he'd decided that the best way to calm his overactive mind was to make his way to sanctuary—Bar-None.

Declan drove over to the bar and walked through the door. Mickey the bartender looked up and smiled, then his brow wrinkled. He held out his hand and without being asked, Declan dropped his car keys into it. Declan had once joked that Mickey should have been in a circus sideshow as a mind reader.

Mickey had said, "I am in a sideshow. Just look around. Beautiful freaks and con-men everywhere."

Declan decided he would sit at the bar with the old-timers who didn't want to bother wasting their time walking all the way from their table to order their next round of Mickey's Magical Memory Erasure. This was precisely where Declan belonged.

Mickey brought him a double vodka. Something was different about Mickey tonight. His hair had changed from its previous blue tones to bright shades of orange and amber that somehow managed to complement his dark eyes. It was like a halo of fall leaves had crowned his head, and on Mickey, it looked good.

After drink two — or was it three? — Declan began to feel his thoughts start to slow down. A young black man in his early thirties sauntered over to the bar. He wore a black mesh shirt that revealed his muscular torso, and tight red jeans that flared at the bottom. He sat beside Declan, who looked at his face through vodka-soaked eyes. The young man had a military buzz-cut and a clean-shaven face. His cheekbones were sharp enough Declan could cut himself on them. And his eyes...he must have been wearing contact lenses because nature didn't make eyes that shade of green.

"You're Declan Hunt, aren't you? Can I buy you a drink?" he said.

Declan nodded his approval.

The man looked down the long bar and raised his hand. Declan knew that guys this beautiful didn't have to go through the motions that mortal men did, just to get a bartender's attention. Eyes were always on them.

The man turned back to Declan. "I wanted to thank you. You may not remember me, but you helped out a friend of mine on a case of a rather personal nature, and it made a huge difference to his life."

The man placed his hand on Declan's thigh and started to slide it up until he reached the detective's crotch.

Declan looked at him.

The man massaged Declan into a rock-hard mass in spite of his drunken state. Every part of Declan's body was telling him to drag this guy to the washroom, throw him into a stall and ride him like a cowboy.

Just then, on the bar in front of him, Declan's phone chirped with a text. He glanced down and could just make out the words. It was from Charlie.

Sorry I was so angry last night. See you on Monday.

Declan stood and, without saying a word, left the building. He staggered out onto the street, and was narrowly missed by a passing cab that blared out from the darkness and sent him reeling back onto the sidewalk.

He made his way to nowhere in particular.

A voice rang out in his head. *You're doing it again. Sabotaging yourself, just like you always do when things are looking good because you know that you don't deserve good things to happen to you. You don't like when your emotions aren't under control. Bad things happen when you get out of control.*

A panhandler on the street asked Declan for a cigarette.

If you do something good, then it undoes the bad.

Declan reached into his pocket and pulled out a bunch of bills and stuffed them into the guy's hand.

"Thanks, buddy," the guy called out, his voice barely penetrating the fog of Declan's mind as he stumbled along his way. His feet took him along the well-worn path that led to momentary release and, in the end, sadness. He looked up at the front door of The Greek—Calgary's biggest gay bathhouse. It was like a mythical siren that called to lonely, miserable men like Declan Hunt, and crashed them among the rocks.

* * * *

Mickey's cell phone rang. It was two in the morning—closing time. He glanced at it and knew the number.

"Hey, buddy. What's up?" he said.

"I...I need help, Mickey."

It was Declan and he sounded worse than he had in a long time.

"You certainly do, my friend. Stay put and keep your phone on. I'll be there in a few."

Mickey disconnected. He killed the music that was playing over the bar's speaker system.

"Okay, listen up. The joint's closing for the night. Everybody pay what you owe to The Kid here behind the bar. And don't forget to tip him good. He's been slaving all day mopping up your piss and tolerating your grubby hands on his ass."

He looked over at The Kid. "You up to this? I've got an emergency to take care of."

"I got it, boss. I won't let you down."

"I know you won't. And don't forget to lock up, turn on the alarm and head out through the back door."

Mickey took off his apron, went out to the parking lot and hopped into his broken-down army-surplus Jeep. He knew where he'd find Declan.

As he pulled up at The Greek, he spotted his friend sitting on the steps to the bathhouse with Mateo, the night manager. Mateo had probably dialled the phone for Declan.

Mateo waved and said, "Mickey, thanks for coming. I found him sitting out here. He's been on the steps all night. He wouldn't come in. He keeps saying that something's wrong and he feels like he should never go in again. He said he needed your help. He also kept mumbling something about Michael?"

"Thanks, Mateo," Mickey said.

"Do you want a hand?"

"No. I think I have it. Come on, my friend," he said to Declan. "Let's get you off the street."

Mickey wasn't large, but he was strong. He manhandled Declan into the passenger seat of his Jeep. He pulled the seatbelt around him and fastened him in. Declan drunkenly swung his head around to look at him. His eyes were red.

"Man…" Mickey said, "you've got to quit doing this to yourself."

Mickey drove to Declan's apartment and got him upstairs to bed. Before he left, he put a note on his bedside table.

Talk to Michael. Then get off your ass and talk to Charlie. He deserves to know.

Chapter Five

On Monday morning, before Charlie headed up to the office, he poked his nose into Gwen's café.

"You're getting in a little late," she said.

"I was out dancing with Carrie. I have no idea when we actually got in."

"Sunday dancing. Good Lord, what will the youth of today get up to next?"

Gwen rose from her chair and wandered behind the counter. She picked out an almond-encrusted *pain au chocolat*.

"Here. Try one of these. They're something new."

Charlie bit into it and his eyes lit up. "Oh my God. I'll never eat a plain one again."

Gwen smiled. "Now, what can I get you?"

"An extra-large latte with a triple shot of espresso."

"Anything for Declan?"

Charlie paused. *Business as usual.* "A large double-shot Americano, please."

He grabbed the coffees and headed up to the office.

As Charlie got to his desk, he heard the familiar crash of weights hitting the floor of the apartment above. It was leg day for Declan and Charlie knew that meant he'd be doing squats with his barbells.

Crash. Another set done and he'd dropped the weights to the floor.

It's a wonder that any of the ceiling lights in the office still work.

Charlie put on his best smile and headed up the stairs. Declan came into view. He wore nothing but tight workout shorts and training shoes. Charlie remembered once telling Declan that the company had enough money that they could afford a new pair of trainers for him. Declan had said that he had the trainers worked in the way he liked.

Declan's muscles strained as he squatted and hoisted weights that far exceeded his own mass. He bent forward at the waist, keeping his back flat and his head looking straight ahead, watching himself in the mirror. Then he dropped the weights onto the padded floor mat. He paused for a second, looking at the reflection of his body.

Charlie cleared his throat. Declan turned and saw Charlie at the top of the stairs. They stared at each other for an awkward moment.

"I...thought you might want this," Charlie said, offering up the coffee.

"Thanks," Declan replied. The tension was palpable.

Charlie put the coffee on the small kitchen counter.

"I'd better..." Charlie started, pointing to the stairs. "Emails don't answer themselves."

He turned and Declan said "Charlie—"

"Yes," Charlie said, spinning around.

"Thanks for the coffee."

"Yeah. No problem."

Charlie headed down to the office leaving Declan alone. *Fuck.*

As Charlie reached his desk the phone rang. He answered. "Declan Hunt Investigations, Charlie Watts speaking."

"Yeah, ah, may I speak to Mr Hunt, please?"

"I'm afraid he's not in the office at the moment. Perhaps I could help you. I'm Mr Hunt's assistant."

"Um…sure, I guess. Look, I was wondering if Mr Hunt could look into my case. It's a rather personal matter. I think I might be in trouble."

"I see. I'm very sorry to hear that. Why don't I take down your contact information and I'll have Mr Hunt get in touch with you when he comes in?"

"I've been told I can trust him. I just don't know what I'll do if…" Their voice started to crack.

Charlie said, "You've come to the right place. I assure you." Charlie noted the name and phone number of the potential new client, finishing with, "I promise he'll get back to you as soon as he can."

As Charlie disconnected, he heard, "Once again, you are a life-saver."

He turned. Declan was leaning out of his office doorway with his coffee in hand. He still wore nothing but his shorts, shoes and sweat. He hoisted his coffee cup.

Just remember, Charlie thought, *business as usual.*

"I just had a call from a Cody White. He wants to talk to you. Here's his number."

Charlie brought the message to Declan, who met him halfway. Declan took the piece of paper. Charlie stood less than a foot away from the detective. He took a deep breath in, trapping the scent of the man who, moments ago, had made him feel weak in the knees in spite of himself.

As Declan scanned the message, his cell phone buzzed. "Can you give Cody a call back and tell him I've been delayed and will get back to him as soon as I can. I have an important meeting I have to get to."

"I don't have anything in the office calendar. Did I miss something?" Charlie asked.

"No. I didn't put it in the calendar. It's personal," Declan said.

"Oh. Okay," Charlie said, trying not to sound hurt.

"I'm going to go take a shower. By the way, I've been thinking about that Yamada guy from the party the other night. There's something not sitting right with me about his story. Could you write up anything you remember from our meeting and see if you can dig anything up on him? And while you're at it, see what you can find out about Malcolm Tull."

"Sure," Charlie said.

"I'll text you when I'm done and maybe we can grab a drink and you can fill me in. We can meet at Bar-None around five-thirty if that's okay with you."

"Sounds great."

And maybe you can fill me in on your mysterious meeting that isn't in your calendar.

Chapter Six

Charlie arrived at the bar right on time and looked for Declan, but he wasn't there. Charlie watched Mickey the bartender drop off a couple of mixed drinks to a young couple at one of the window tables. He couldn't help but smile. The pair appeared to be in their early twenties and were pawing at each other like two newlyweds.

As Mickey walked back to the bar, he said, "I think your date's here."

Charlie turned to see Declan coming through the door. He had a troubled look on his face.

What's he been up to?

"Sorry I took so long," Declan said with a weary smile. "Where do you want to sit?"

Charlie led Declan to a table near the front window beside the two young lovers, where the natural light filtered in through the windows. Mickey followed them and asked, "The usual?"

"Yes, please," Charlie replied.

Declan just nodded.

"So, tell me what you've found out," Declan said.

"Well," Charlie started as he opened his laptop, "this is turning out to be more interesting than I thought. First, I looked into Sinclair Yamada. He's thirty-three years old, single, born and raised in Halifax, Nova Scotia. He has a master's degree from Harvard and started work as an editor at Mount Temple Press in 2014. He's written a dozen essays on the history of the treatment of the Japanese in Canada, which have been published in *The Globe and Mail*, *Maclean's* and the *Canadian Historical Review*, but has not ventured into fiction."

"And that's interesting?" Declan asked. "Anything else on him?"

"Only that he's a top-level cricket player with a membership at the Glenmore Cricket Club," Charlie said looking up at Declan, shrugging his shoulders. "Who knew we had a cricket club?" He focused back on the laptop. "He has a Facebook and Instagram page but he appears to have abandoned his X account after posting a nasty comment about Elon Musk."

Charlie paused as Mickey dropped off their drinks at the table. "Thanks, Mickey."

"That's it?" Declan asked as he took a swig from his drink.

"In a way, that's what's interesting. He feels a little too normal. I went as deep as I could on the internet — places you don't want to know about — and found nothing. His remaining social media accounts are restricted to publishing, cricket and the occasional funny animal videos. He's just a normal guy — who looks pretty hot in a Speedo, by the way."

"Please tell me that's not everything."

"Oh, have a little more faith in me," Charlie replied,

smiling. "Next I started looking into the late Mr Tull. I discovered that he wrote a well-received first novel that was published by Mount Temple Press. Since he took over from Thomas Pritchard at Hoodoo House in 2008, he's only written four books, and they've been mediocre mystery novels. I checked the sales rankings of the books on Amazon and they're in the basement. Not a good showing for being basically on salary for fifteen years. My question is why would Mount Temple Press publish them? They promote themselves as Canada's pre-eminent publisher of history, art and *literary* fiction, but mystery is a bit outside of their usual catalogue."

Charlie took a swig of his beer.

"Maybe they just had to put the books out to justify expenses for the foundation?" Declan offered.

"Possibly. But why keep on someone who's only a passable writer? They could have ditched him at any time."

"From what we know about him, maybe he had something on someone in the foundation," Declan replied.

"It also got me wondering about Tull's predecessor, Thomas Pritchard. He was there from 1988 until his death in 2008. Guess how many of his books he published before landing the spot as first writer-in-residence?"

"Not a clue."

"The only book I found that was written by Thomas Pritchard before moving into Hoodoo House was published in 1985. A science-fiction fantasy called *The World Before Time*. Again — don't you think it's kinda weird that they would choose to support a writer like that? Not art, not history and definitely not literary fiction."

"Aren't we being judgmental?" Declan said, smiling.

"I'm just saying science-fiction fantasy also seems a little out of place in their catalogue. The other thing about Pritchard is that during his twenty years with the foundation he published" — Charlie paused for effect — "*one* book!"

Charlie said this loudly enough that the young couple sitting next to them jumped.

"Sorry," Charlie said in a hushed tone. "Just one book. No other short stories or essays. Nothing."

Declan sat back and took another sip of his scotch.

"It must have been a masterpiece."

Charlie shook his head. "Not really. The critics called it long-winded and overly prosaic. It was six hundred pages long, but from what I read, it wasn't something that you would think would take twenty years to write."

"That is interesting. You know, you're really good at this."

"Thank you," Charlie said, taking a seated bow.

Declan nursed his drink for a moment before asking, "Could the publisher be involved in a tax scam?"

"A question for Mr Attwal, maybe?" Charlie asked.

"Maybe…"

"Anyway, this all got me wondering about Mount Temple Press. They are not as big a player as they used to be. They once represented several high-level Canadian novelists — ones you probably studied in high school."

"Oh God."

"Don't worry. They're mostly all dead now. There are rumours all over the literary sites that Mount Temple's been looking for takeover bids from the remaining big players."

"If they aren't a heavy hitter, why would anyone want to buy them?" Declan asked.

"Because they still have one money-making property — *The Heart's Shadow* series of romance novels written by Marjorie Ellis."

"Romance novels? And that counts as literary fiction?" Declan said, raising his eyebrows.

"The first book in the series was more along the line of a Jane Austen novel. And money talks. There have been over thirty novels in the series and they've brought millions of dollars into the Mount Temple coffers. It's this series that provides the funding for the Heart's Shadow Foundation which, in turn, pays the salaries of the writers like Tull and the cost of running Hoodoo House."

"Interesting."

Mickey interrupted with another round of drinks.

Declan chewed his lip and drummed his fingers on the table. "So we've got a foundation that might be involved in a tax scam, Thomas Pritchard who was apparently paid for twenty years to write one book and the latest writer who mysteriously died at a time when he was blackmailing his editor."

Charlie nodded and said, "A lot more to this case than a missing computer with a manuscript and sex videos on it."

Declan turned his head towards the young couple beside them who were clearly eavesdropping. "I'd suggest you turn your ears the other way. And if I find that you've breathed a single word of this on social media, I will have my assistant hunt down all of the embarrassing naked images of yourselves that you've been sharing with each other and make sure your contacts see each and every one of them."

The two got up at once and moved to the back of the bar.

Charlie laughed. "It's not quite that easy."

Declan shrugged. "They don't need to know that."

"So what's our next move?" Charlie asked.

"I think it's time for a visit to Hoodoo House. It's the last place Tull was seen alive and if he hid the computer, it might be there. Can you get in touch with Yamada and set it up?"

"Sure. And what if the computer was stolen?"

Declan finished his drink. "Maybe someone at the house saw something that can point us in the right direction."

He pulled out his phone and checked the time. "Let's call it quits for the day. I'm going to the washroom. If Mickey comes by, tell him to put it on my tab."

Declan set his phone down on the table and made his way to the back of the bar. Just as he walked into the washroom, his phone buzzed. Charlie glanced at the screen. There was a text from someone named Michael. The text preview said '*Thanks for this afternoon.*'

Charlie pondered the message.

It's none of my business.

When Declan returned, Charlie said nothing.

Declan picked up his phone without looking at it and said, "So, see you at nine tomorrow?"

"As usual," Charlie replied. "I gotta go."

Who the fuck is Michael?

Chapter Seven

Henry was working on a math assignment in the kitchen when the phone rang. He usually wouldn't answer it. That was Gramma Carol's job, and he knew it wouldn't be for him. He never got phone calls.

After the second ring, Henry remembered that the answering machine wasn't going to pick up because it had been broken when Mr Tull had thrown it across the room last month. Henry decided he'd better answer the phone so that it wouldn't wake Gramma Carol up from her afternoon nap.

"Good afternoon, Henry Quill speaking. How may I direct your call?"

"Is Malcolm Tull in?" a deep voice at the other end of the line asked. "I need to speak with him. It's urgent."

It had been over a week since Mr Tull's body had been discovered in the writing room and Henry decided that the truth was the easiest way to deal with the caller.

"Mr Tull's dead. Can I help you?"

There was silence on the line then the caller

disconnected.

"Huh. Rude," Henry said to himself as he hung up the phone.

Two math questions later, the phone rang again. Henry answered. He thought he'd handled the first call quite professionally and perhaps Gramma Carol would let him become the official Hoodoo House receptionist. He could use the salary. Comic book prices were going up, after all.

"Good afternoon, Hoodoo House, Henry Quill speaking. How may I direct your call?"

"Henry. What are you doing answering the phone?" It was Mr Yamada.

"Gramma Carol's lying down for her afternoon nap and the answering machine's still broken."

"Look, would you let her know that a private detective named Declan Hunt will be coming by? I've hired him to look into Mr Tull's missing computer. This is important, Henry, because it has files on it that belong to Mount Temple Press. I want to make sure Mr Hunt gets all of the assistance he needs. Tell Mrs Cameron to allow him full access to the house and answer any of his questions."

"Okay. No problem," Henry replied.

"Did you get all that?"

"Yup. I've got it," Henry answered, trying not to sound annoyed.

There was a pause on the phone, then Mr Yamada said, "Maybe you should wake Mrs Cameron up so I can talk to her."

Henry sighed. "There's a detective named Declan Hunt coming to the house to find Mr Tull's computer and we are to help him with anything he needs. I can remember that, Mr Yamada. And I'm sure Gramma Carol will call you if she has any questions. Now, if there's nothing else, I have the mathematical probability of independent events to get back to."

After Mr Yamada hung up, Henry tried to return to his homework, but he couldn't focus. He'd never met a real private detective before. He wondered if he was like any of the ones Henry had seen in his comic books. And what would he ask?

Henry stared at the math problems on the table. They became less interesting the more he thought about the detective and what he was coming to look for — Mr Tull's computer. Where could it be? Somewhere in the house? Maybe Henry could find it first. He knew Hoodoo House better than anyone. And Gramma Carol would be asleep for at least another half an hour. Maybe he should do a little sleuthing. If he found the computer before the detective got here, maybe Mr Yamada would give him a reward.

Henry decided to start in the writing room. The door had been kept closed since the police had removed the body of Mr Tull, and Gramma Carol had scoured the place with a strong cleaning solution in order to remove any trace of what had happened. Henry entered and quietly closed the door behind him.

He looked around the room. It appeared to be exactly as it had been before Mr Tull's death. Henry made his way to the desk and checked the desk drawers. They were locked, but he knew that Mr Tull had kept the key tucked inside a book called *The Keys of the Kingdom*. Henry knew a lot of things about Mr Tull.

He retrieved the key and opened the desk drawers but nothing was out of place. Henry was certain since he knew where everything was supposed to be.

Mr Tull's bedroom was next to be searched, even though Henry knew the police had been through it. He looked everywhere, including under the dresser drawers, behind the framed prints on the walls, even under the mattress and the bed itself, tugging away at the fabric that sealed the bottom of the box spring just in case Mr Tull had slid something in there, like Henry had done in his own room with his memory box — but he found nothing.

That left only one more place to look — the basement…and the tunnel.

Henry crept down the stairs to the main floor. Over the years he had mapped out in his mind which stairs to avoid if he didn't want the squeak of a loose tread to cut through the house. Once he'd reached the main floor in safety, he crept down the hall and opened the cellar door, then turned on the light and descended into the basement.

The cellar was large, damp and lined with shelves. There wasn't much stored there, but what there was, Gramma Carol kept on the shelves near the foot of the stairs. She hated to go down to the basement. There were all sorts of bugs down there which freaked her out. Henry found this strange because nothing else seemed to frighten her. Henry liked insects. Whenever he heard Gramma Carol shriek in another room, he'd come running. Before she could get the broom to swat the insects to heaven, Henry would come to their rescue, scoop them up into his hands and rush them outside to safety. But today wasn't about bugs — Henry was on a sleuthing mission.

First he examined the shelves to see if anything had been moved, but it all looked pretty much the same as usual. *No computer here*.

He made his way towards the wall of shelves farthest from the stairs. It had a gap beside and behind it wide enough for a person to slip through. No one would ever notice it unless they got up beside the shelf because the light from the single bulb in the ceiling didn't reach to the far corner.

Henry aimed for the gap and rounded the corner. Behind the shelves there was an archway built into the stone wall of the basement which led to a hallway, though it was more of a tunnel with rough wooden walls and a packed dirt floor. Henry followed it to the end and came to a door made of slats of wood that he knew opened onto the coulee behind the house. There was still no sign of the computer.

As he retraced his steps, Henry thought back to the day before Mr Tull was found dead. Henry had planned on taking a shortcut through the tunnel out to the coulee. At the top of the stairs to the cellar, he'd heard two voices. One of them had been Mr Tull's and the other one certainly hadn't been Gramma Carol. Her voice wasn't that deep. Henry didn't remember anyone else coming in through the front door, so the other person must have come in through the tunnel.

As Henry had stopped at the top of the stairs to listen that afternoon, the voices had started to fade away. Henry had been curious, so he'd gone down the stairs and slipped into the gap behind the shelves. He'd heard a faint beeping sound. By the time he'd gotten to the tunnel, Mr Tull and the other person had been nowhere in sight. Maybe Mr Tull and his guest had left through the coulee door. Henry had decided to confirm his hunch, but about halfway towards the door, he'd heard a sound coming from behind a section of the wall. One of the vertical boards that separated the wall into sections had been loosened and jutted out at a slight angle. He had reached towards the board, but at that exact moment, Henry had heard a sharp sound, followed by a muffled scream from behind the wall. He'd run back upstairs to his second-floor bedroom and closed his door. He hadn't been back since.

Today, with no Malcolm Tull or friend around, and Gramma Carol sound asleep in her room, Henry felt no fear. He located the vertical board he was looking for and tugged at it. The board came away. It was hinged and when opened revealed a new-looking keypad. Henry knew there must be a room behind the wall. Maybe that was where Mr Tull had left his computer. He punched in as many codes as he could think of, but none of them seemed to work. After ten minutes, Henry gave up and headed back to the kitchen. He decided he wouldn't tell Gramma Carol about this yet. He'd wait until the detective came then reveal what he knew, just like the hero always did in his comic books.

Chapter Eight

It was just after noon when Declan left his office and headed into the main reception area. Charlie was diligently working at his computer.

"Ready to head to Hoodoo House?" Declan asked.

"Sure," Charlie said without looking up. He collected his jacket and put a fistful of notes into his bag. His lips were firmly set in a frown and Declan could see that for some reason, Charlie was avoiding eye contact.

"I think we need something before we start."

Declan led the way downstairs and straight into Gwen's shop. "Two coffees to go, Gwen. And maybe some of those," he said, pointing to the pastries.

That should put a smile on his face.

It didn't.

Once Declan had paid, they made their way to the parking lot and Charlie walked directly to Declan's van. Declan stopped him. "I thought we could take the Beast this time. I haven't had a chance to drive your car yet, and this way you can read me your notes on the way out…if that's okay with you?"

"Sure. No problem," Charlie said, handing him the keys.

Declan sat in the driver's seat and looked for the cup holder. It became clear that cars of this age were not equipped with such luxuries. He passed his coffee cup to Charlie. "Apparently you and your fellow muscle car maniacs don't drink and drive."

Charlie didn't even crack a smile.

They drove in silence through the streets of Calgary and out onto the highway. As they reached the outskirts of town, where city turned to prairie, Charlie finally spoke.

"Who's Michael?"

Declan felt like he'd been caught with his pants down.

"How do you know about Michael?" Declan asked.

"When you went to the washroom at the bar yesterday, you left your phone on the table. A text came in and I glanced over at it. It was from Michael. The text preview said 'Thanks for this afternoon.' I didn't open the text. I wasn't spying on you."

Declan glanced over at him. Charlie was staring forward. His face was tense. Declan wished he could tell him now, tell him everything, but…he wasn't ready.

"Michael's just a friend. That's all."

"Oh," Charlie said. "What kind of friend?"

Charlie was staring at him now.

"It's…just some personal shit. I don't want to talk about it. Let's focus on Hoodoo House. What can you tell me?"

"Fine…strictly business," Charlie said, gritting his teeth, as he reached down and pulled a few pages of notes out of his messenger bag. He riffled through them and stared at his notes as he spoke. "Technically Hoodoo House is owned by the novelist Marjorie Ellis, who wrote the famous novel *The Ragtag Crew*. It was a huge hit. They did a film of the book that was nominated for an Oscar. *The Ragtag Crew* made Marjorie Ellis and her publisher Mount Temple Press millions of dollars."

Declan nodded. "So you make millions of dollars. Why buy a property on the edge of the Badlands in Alberta?"

Charlie continued, "There's a bit of mystique surrounding the author. When her novel came out, it was released with a female silhouette instead of a photo, and no bio. Apparently Marjorie Ellis is a recluse and insisted that the only identity attached to the book would be her name. From what I could find out, she purchased Hoodoo House in 1981 as a place out of the public eye. And nobody really knew who she was. The purchase agreement was done through Mount Temple Press so her name wouldn't be exposed to the real-estate company."

"So why isn't she living there now?" Declan asked.

Charlie reached down and took a sip of his coffee, then continued. "According to my research, after the huge success of her first novel, her second novel was a flop. It came out in 1983 and was called *The Offal House* — that's offal as in o-f-f-a-l, not a-w-f-u-l. They made a film of the second book, but it was a bust. It lost a ton of money and the novel itself never took off. Rumour has it that this didn't sit well with the mysterious author and she had some sort of breakdown and moved to Portugal."

Declan frowned. "But why not just sell the house?"

"Maybe she thought she'd come back some day. All I know is that the house itself became famous after she left when people found out she'd lived there. And Portugal must agree with her because that's where she began *The Heart's Shadow* series, which is up to thirty-one books now. My mom's read every single one of them. That series has turned a good profit, and with that money she established the Heart's Shadow Foundation to support authors of interest to her publisher. And as you know, at this point there have only been two of them — Thomas Pritchard and Malcolm Tull."

Declan glanced over at Charlie. "Anything else?"

Charlie shuffled the remainder of his papers, then handed Declan his lukewarm coffee. "Not really. Maybe we'll find out more when we get there."

Declan swigged back the drink, went to toss it on the floor then thought better of it and returned the empty cup back to Charlie.

They continued on in silence.

Declan drove the car around a corner and turned from Township Road 271A onto a small concession road, taking in the waving fields of golden crops, dappled by the shadows of the clouds that sailed through the blue prairie sky which stretched from horizon to horizon.

"What are they growing there?" Charlie asked.

Declan was happy Charlie had broken the silence.

"I think it's durum wheat," Declan said. "The stuff pasta's made out of. If you look over there, you can see the swaths cut in the fields where they've started harvesting."

"Huh."

"We'll make a country boy out of you yet," Declan joked.

"Says the guy who rarely leaves the city unless he's forced to," Charlie said, as he checked his phone for directions. "According to Sinclair's instructions, we should almost be there."

The road curved to the west around a hill.

"There," Declan said.

At the top of a hill to the east, on a flat, elevated plane between the road and what must have been a drop-off, sat the large, two-storey clapboard structure.

They pulled into the gravel drive which curved up to the house. Declan stared at a tall, thin spire of stone, capped with a flat rock which rose in front of the house.

Hoodoo House. More like the House on Haunted Hill.

Chapter Nine

Charlie and Declan mounted the old wooden stairs. Along the side of the porch was a two-person swing. Charlie noticed a few comic books on it weighted down with a rock, presumably so they wouldn't blow away. Declan pressed the old brass doorbell button, but Charlie didn't hear anything. Declan looked at him, shrugged then reached up for the brass knocker, but before he could knock, the door opened. A woman who looked not quite as old as Charlie's Gran stood there, looking slightly put out.

"You must be the detective," she said. "Well—come in." She stepped aside and closed the door as soon as they had crossed the threshold.

"I'm Mrs Cameron, the housekeeper here at Hoodoo House."

"Thank you for allowing us to visit, Mrs Cameron," Declan replied. "I'm Declan Hunt and this is my assistant Charlie Watts."

Charlie reached out and said, "Pleased to meet you."

Mrs Cameron quickly gripped his hand in hers, then released it just as fast. Charlie could feel the callouses of hands that were used to hard work.

"We just wanted to ask some questions about Mr Tull and see if you can help shed some light on his missing computer," Declan continued.

"I'm not sure what I can offer you," she replied. "The police have already questioned me, but I'll help if I can."

Charlie turned his attention to his surroundings. With the door closed, it took a moment to grow accustomed to the dark interior. The floors, doors and walls were all in dark-stained wood, as was the staircase leading upstairs. The interior main hallway of Hoodoo House was not only isolated from the light of the prairie sky, but it was also shut off from the sounds of the outdoors — the whisper of the wind, the birds and the insects all seemed to cease to exist once they had crossed the threshold. It was a house overflowing with a powerful silence.

They walked down the long dim hallway. Charlie felt the house was somehow closing in around him, like it was trying to swallow him. It made him uneasy. He glanced back over his right shoulder.

"Feel like you're being watched?" Mrs Cameron asked him.

"Yes." Charlie said.

"This place has that effect on most visitors until they get used to it. Must be something in the architecture that does it, or the way the air moves through the house."

The mood was broken by the galumphing sound of someone coming rapidly down the stairs.

"Are you the detective?" a young boy asked.

Mrs Cameron replied, "Slow down, young man. This is Mr Hunt and his assistant Charlie Watts." She turned back towards the two men, "And this is Henry, my ward. He lives in the house with me and I take care of him."

Declan reached out his hand. "Pleasure to meet you, Henry. You can call me Declan if you want."

"There was an Irish saint named Declan, or probably more likely Deaglán. He founded a monastery in Ireland in the fifth century. It's a good name," Henry replied.

Charlie smiled. It was clear the boy was bright.

"I read a lot," he continued.

"Now Henry, don't be a bother," Mrs Cameron said. "These men have come to ask some questions about Mr Tull. Gentlemen, if you would follow me."

Henry interjected, "What do you think of Hoodoo House? They say there's a ghost here from a lady who died when it was a hotel. She was a prostitute."

"Henry, that's enough," Mrs Cameron scolded as they reached the brightly lit room at the end of the hallway — the kitchen.

Charlie noted it had a different energy, more like it was the heart of the house.

"You might as well sit," Mrs Cameron said. "I just made a pot of tea. Would you like some?"

Declan smiled. "That would be wonderful, Mrs Cameron. Thank you."

"I'd love one too," Charlie added. "Thanks."

She plunked a teapot, four mugs and a plate of cookies down on the large kitchen table, followed by a sugar bowl with a spoon in it and a small pitcher of milk.

"I don't have any teacups. Mugs'll have to do," she warned. "And Henry — don't eat all of the cookies. Leave some for our guests."

Charlie looked over. The boy already had one cookie in his mouth and another in his hand. With half a cookie still in his mouth, Henry tugged on Declan's sleeve and said, "Do you want me to take you on a tour of the house? There's some things I want to show you. Did you know that the premier of Alberta came here once—"

"Henry," Mrs Cameron interrupted, "leave the man alone."

Henry's face fell.

"Maybe Henry could show *me* around the house," Charlie offered. "Having a good look around might help with the case and it would give you two a chance to talk."

"Can I?" Henry asked Mrs Cameron, regaining some of his enthusiasm.

"All right," she said. "But try not to talk his ear off."

"Come on," Henry said, jumping up from his chair and exiting the kitchen.

Charlie glanced at Declan and Mrs Cameron, shrugged his shoulders then quickly followed Henry back down the main hallway.

"So, you're not a detective?" Henry asked

"No. I'm his assistant."

"What does that mean?"

"I'm the man behind the detective—the guy who cracks the codes for him. The one who works silently in the background, hacking his way into people's computers to find out their secrets."

Henry stared at him, his mouth open. "That is so cool!"

As they walked towards the front of the house, Charlie looked more closely at the hall and noted that there were doors which opened to the left and the right.

"There's only a few small rooms on the main floor. The first two are Gramma Carol's bedroom and a bathroom on the other side. The back of the house, where we just came from, is of course the kitchen. And at the front of the house are the two really big rooms. That's what I'd like to show you first."

At the foot of the stairs, to the left of the main door, Henry led Charlie through a dark oak archway covered by faded red velvet curtains. Henry parted the curtains to reveal a large room. It was empty except for a large table set up near the far window. Henry took Charlie straight to it. On top of the table was a jigsaw puzzle. What was strange was that it was upside-down with the backing of the puzzle facing upwards.

"I see you like doing jigsaw puzzles," Charlie said. "Do you play them like that to make it more challenging?"

"It's easier this way." Henry leaned in towards Charlie. "Sometimes, if it's picture side up, I spend so much time looking at the bit of the picture I've assembled that I never get around to finishing it. Gramma Carol said if I do it this way, I can focus better… I have issues."

"You're not the only one," Charlie said with a wink before sitting down across from him.

Henry began working on the puzzle, taking pieces and expertly fitting them into place.

Charlie said, "So, Mrs Cameron takes care of you?"

"Yeah. My mom's dead. Gramma Carol was a good friend of my Gramma Rachael who took care of me after my mom died. And then when Gramma Rachael got sick and was dying, Gramma Carol said she would take care of me. I think Gramma Carol and Gramma Rachael used to be more than friends, if you know what

I mean. Gramma Carol's also my teacher. I don't think like other kids, so it's easier if I'm homeschooled."

In the corner of the room, Charlie spied a stack of comic books. "It looks like you're a fan of comics."

Henry's eyes lit up. "They're the best! Do you like them too?"

"I used to love them when I was your age," Charlie replied.

"Which did you like?"

"I'd have to say Spider-Man was my favourite. I used to fantasize about swinging from tall buildings, which was weird because I was terrified of heights."

Henry laughed.

"How about you?" Charlie asked.

Henry dove for the stack of comic books and shoved one at Charlie. "This is my favourite. *Momrath and The Slithe*. Do you know it?"

"No. Is it new?"

"It's been around forever. Five years, at least."

Henry flipped open the comic and thrust it into Charlie's face. It showed a picture of a slim character, dressed all in black. He stood, legs spread apart, arms straight out from his sides. In one hand was a black *bo* staff, the weapon of a martial arts specialist. He faced a huge, muscled goliath.

"That's Momrath," Henry said, pointing to the giant brute. "And that's The Slithe," he said of the slim man in black. "He was Marty Finn, a mail clerk working at a chemical production factory who came across Momrath during a break-in. Momrath threw him into an experimental chemical vat. Well, you know the way it always goes. Powerless kid gets super-human powers and tries to hunt down the man who turned him into a superhero."

"Comics are amazing, aren't they?" Charlie said.

"I hope to get a job working in a comic-book store when I get a bit older. But there isn't one in Rosebud, and Drumheller's a bit too far for me to get to. I love to draw my own comics, too. I'm hoping to get good enough to get them published."

Henry slid a few pages at Charlie, who glanced at them. Henry was creating his own *Momrath and The Slithe* comic books.

"These are good," he told Henry.

Charlie knew he was no farther ahead in terms of finding out anything useful about Malcolm Tull and he needed to move the conversation in a different direction.

"Henry, I've come here with Declan to learn more about this old house and the writers who lived here. Are you going to take me on the rest of the tour now?"

"Is Declan your boyfriend?"

Charlie paused. "What? Uh…no."

"Just wondering. I was watching him just after you came in. He looks at you funny. I sense things. He thinks you're special. I just know it."

Charlie tried to keep his expression neutral, and redirected the conversation. "So…do you have someone special that you like?"

"Nah. The only person around here is Gramma Carol and I think she's a bit old for me." Henry laughed.

"It must get lonely out here in the country," Charlie said. "Aside from you and Gramma Carol, was Mr Tull the only other person who stayed here?"

Henry shook his head. "We had visitors, but they never stayed. It was supposed to be a quiet place for the writer."

"And did you know the writer who died?"

"There've been *two* who died here, but Mr Pritchard, he was the first one, he died before I came here. I knew Mr Tull...sort of."

"Did you like him?"

Henry went back to the puzzle, picking up a piece and trying to fit it in place. "He wasn't very nice. He was always telling me off whenever I'd do things. He wouldn't let me in the writing room unless I was bringing him something. Apparently I couldn't even do that right. And..."

Henry stopped. Charlie sensed Henry was uncomfortable with the subject of Mr Tull.

"He doesn't sound like a very nice man."

Henry looked at Charlie. "I don't think he liked people very much. He kept himself locked up in the writing room except when he joined us in the kitchen to eat. Even then, he'd usually take his food back to his room."

"Maybe he was just busy writing and didn't want to be disturbed?"

"All I know is that when he shut the door, no one was allowed to bother him. That was the rule. I broke the rule once and he threw a coffee mug at me. Just about took my head off."

"Why did you go in?"

"Gramma Carol asked me to take him some dessert. But I showed him. I took it up to my bedroom and ate it myself." Henry went back to the puzzle and started to search for another piece to add. He became quiet.

Charlie didn't know what to do next, so he said, "Well, thanks for the tour."

Henry replied, "Oh there's more things to show you, but I was going to wait for the detective."

Charlie raised an eyebrow. "Well, perhaps you can

show me first, and then if it seems important, we can get the detective to check it out."

Henry stared at Charlie for a moment, then said, "Maybe. But you have to promise to show Declan what we've found."

"I promise," Charlie said.

Henry looked across to the velvet curtain. "First I have to give you the rest of the tour." He got up and led Charlie out of the velvet-curtained room and across to the other side of the hall where they entered the second large space at the front of the house.

Henry said, pointing, "This is the writing room where Mr Tull died."

"Would you mind if I took a few quick pictures of the space?" Charlie asked.

"The police already took some pictures."

"It might help with our investigation," Charlie explained.

Henry nodded. "Okay, but make it quick. The other things I want to show you are way more interesting."

Chapter Ten

Declan took a sip of his tea.

"Henry must be quite a handful," he said. "You said he was your ward. Are you two related in any way?"

Mrs Cameron retrieved a kettle and added more hot water to the teapot on the kitchen table. "No, but his grandmother was a good friend of mine."

"How did he wind up here?"

She stared hard at him, then took a sip of her tea. "Do you have anyone in your life that you would do anything for?"

Declan thought about Charlie and said, "Yes. I do."

"Well, I felt that way about Henry's grandmother Rachael. There's no shame in telling you now that we were more than friends when we were younger. But then things changed."

"What things?" Declan asked.

"She wanted children, and we couldn't do that together in those days. She got married and so did I."

"Is Mr Cameron still alive?"

"He died...must be twenty years ago. And Rachael's

husband is dead too. He was a mean man. The only good thing to come out of their marriage was a child late in her life, Henry's mother. I'll be truthful, when he passed away, I didn't feel any sorrow."

Declan continued, "So what happened to Henry's parents?"

"They were killed in a car accident when Henry was four. Rachael took in the boy, but her health declined a few years after. And that's when she came to me to ask if I would look after him. He was nine at the time."

"And the foundation was all right with him staying here?" Declan asked.

"I made my case. I cover his expenses and the foundation allows him to live here as long as he stays out of the writer's hair."

"He seems like a bright kid."

Mrs Cameron smiled. "He is, and he's the best thing about Hoodoo House."

Her careworn face suggested she'd been through a lot in her life. To Declan, she looked like a tough old bird and probably wouldn't be offended if he'd said so.

"What are you grinning at?" she asked, with a perplexed look.

"I was looking at you and thinking how much you remind me of my stepmother."

"A stepmother? Do I look that evil?"

"No, and neither does she. I'd say forceful was a better description of her."

She sat back down. "I hope you don't think it rude that I served your tea in a mug. Someone in the house broke all of the teacups."

"No problem. Teacups don't fit well in these anyway," Declan said, holding up his large, rough hands.

She narrowed her lips and nodded. "Looks like those hands have seen some action."

"This whole body's seen more than what's good for it," he replied.

"I know that feeling," she said, rolling up her sleeve and showing off a ten-centimetre scar that ran up her forearm.

Declan detected the slightest of smiles on her face. "Ouch. That must have hurt."

"Got it caught on a length of barbwire. They wanted me to go to a hospital, but I just washed it up and stitched it myself. More tea?" she asked.

"Please," he said. He took a sip. "Honestly, I think this is the best tea I've ever had."

"Mr Pritchard used to order it in from a small shop in Ladysmith on Vancouver Island. I've just sort of stuck with it."

"He was one of the writers-in-residence, wasn't he?" Declan asked.

"He was. And a wonderful gentleman to boot."

"How long did you know him?"

"Well, let's see," she pondered. "Thomas started in 1988, I believe, and I was hired on a year later."

Declan could see her relaxing. "So, you didn't work for Marjorie Ellis?"

"No, I never had the pleasure. Thomas came to Hoodoo House after the foundation that runs this place was established, and I was hired to help keep the place in order. He was a good man but just couldn't keep house to save his life."

Declan smiled. "It must have been hard when he passed," he said.

She nodded.

"And was Mr Pritchard followed immediately by

Mr Tull?"

"Too soon after, if you ask me."

Declan noticed a change in her demeanour. "And how did working for him compare to Mr Pritchard?"

"I didn't *work* for Thomas. At least it never felt like it. With Mr Tull it was all work, and not pleasant work at that."

"How would you describe him?" Declan inquired.

She laughed. "He was a miserable bastard and I can't say that I'm sorry he's gone. I don't think that man enjoyed much of anything."

"Surely he enjoyed writing?" Declan asked.

"Well, he constantly complained about his publisher and editor —"

"The editor being Mr Yamada?"

She nodded. "Yes. They fought often, and their last fight was a doozy."

"Do you know what the fight was about?"

"I couldn't make it out clearly. From the sound of his voice, Mr Tull had been drinking and was in a foul mood. I can't remember exactly how the argument started, but I distinctly remember hearing Mr Yamada yell something about Mr Tull turning something over to him. Mr Tull said he would make Mr Yamada pay — and no, I wasn't listening at the door. They were yelling so loudly you probably could have heard them from the road."

"What happened next?"

"Mr Yamada stormed out."

Declan nodded. "Do you remember when this happened?" Declan asked.

"Of course. It was the evening before Mr Tull's body was discovered."

Interesting. Yamada never mentioned the fight.

Declan noticed that Mrs Cameron's mug was empty. He picked up the teapot and asked, "May I fill you up?"

"Thank you," she replied.

"So, it appears Mr Tull didn't have a lot of fans," he said with a smile.

"He was nothing but a schoolyard bully. Someone should have put him over their knee and given him a good spanking years ago. And it's not the way he treated me, or the folks from the foundation—we can all take care of ourselves—but his total lack of respect for Marjorie Ellis and her work, work which put a roof over his head and food in his stomach... Well, there was no call for that."

"I take it you're a big fan of Marjorie Ellis?"

Mrs Cameron nodded enthusiastically. "She's a great writer. I'd say one of the best this country has produced. You can't clump her work, at least the earlier novels, with those run-of-the-mill romances that come out these days. Hers have substance and depth, and she's a master of character development. *The Ragtag Crew* was a masterpiece. She should have won that Booker Prize. Her second book, *The Offal House*...well, it seemed a bit rushed. I don't agree with the critics who said it was 'the sophomore curse'. I suspect the publisher pushed her to finish it so he could take advantage of the popularity of the first novel. In my opinion, great books need time to develop. That's probably the only thing Mr Tull and I agreed on, as he certainly took his sweet time writing his novels, but his books were never great like Marjorie Ellis'."

"This is very helpful Mrs Cameron. A few last things. When was the last time you saw Malcolm Tull with his computer?"

She tilted her head. "The last I saw of it, I'd guess, was a few days before he died. He was using it in the writing room."

"Did you see it there on the day before he died?" Declan asked.

She shook her head. "Not that I recall."

"And you didn't think that was strange?"

"Mr Tull, like all writers, I suppose, had his own process. He didn't always write on the computer. Sometimes he did his notes by hand."

"Thank you. Now tell me, did Mr Tull have friends or other people who visited him while he was here?"

She sat for a moment, chewing on her bottom lip before continuing, "He had visits from strange people."

"Strange in what way?"

"Disreputable. From time to time, rough-looking young men would show up at the house, and at all hours of the day and night. I didn't approve, but I don't own the house, so it isn't my business, I suppose."

"And did any of these people visit him on the day before he was found dead?" Declan asked.

"I didn't see anybody, but there was a large Harley parked at the side of the house for a few hours that afternoon," she replied, "and I suspect whoever was riding that bike was up to no good."

Chapter Eleven

Charlie finished taking pictures of the writing room, the desk and the bookcases around it on his phone.

Henry said, "Come on outside. I want to tell you about the history of the house."

Charlie followed Henry, who barely took a breath between sentences as he began what seemed to be a well-rehearsed patter.

"Construction of Hoodoo House, which was originally called the Coulee Hotel, began in 1918. It was built during the Alberta Prohibition as a secret drinking establishment and brothel. The owners knew that it might be raided by police so it was built with a secret emergency exit for those in the know.

"As you can see, the building is topped by an observation tower which allowed for lookouts to keep their eyes peeled for approaching lawmen. It was eventually closed down by the police for being a house of ill repute. In the nineteen-fifties, the hotel was purchased by Lazlo Spence, an eccentric artist and wannabe hotel owner, who constructed several haphazard additions, adding ten more rooms. He also created the twenty-foot-high sculpture at the front which is called 'Spirit of the Hoodoo'. That's when the building became Hoodoo House. The hotel went bankrupt in the late nineteen-seventies and stood abandoned until the Heart's Shadow Foundation bought it on Miss Ellis' behalf."

Charlie said, "Where did you learn all of this?"

"Gramma Carol taught me. It's useful information for when I'm giving tours."

"You give tours? To who?" Charlie asked.

"To *whom*," Henry replied.

Mrs Cameron was obviously a good teacher.

"Well, they aren't official tours, but you see, Miss Ellis, who was the first writer in the house, has lots of fans. They come from all over the world to pay homage to her because she wrote a famous book called *The Ragtag Crew*, and she also has fans for *The Heart's Shadow* series.

"Last year I had a small bus come by with tourists from Japan. I took them on a tour around the outside of the house telling them everything I could remember about it. I even included a few things about when this was a place for gambling and was filled with women of ill-repute. That's the polite term for hookers. So anyway, I made up this story that this is where the Premier of Alberta was almost arrested when the police raided the place. And they believed it! They tipped me twice what I normally charge for a tour."

"Did you ever make up stories about Mr Tull, or Miss Ellis or their books?"

Henry's eyes widened. "No. It's important to honour Miss Ellis' legacy. After all, because of her, I have a place to live. At least that's what Gramma Carol says."

"So, people pay you for taking them through the house?"

"I'm not allowed to take them into the house. Mr Tull would have had a shit-fit if I'd done that. I just walk people around the outside. I let them peek in through the kitchen and puzzle room windows. Gramma Carol says as long as I don't take them inside or disturb the writer, I'm allowed to do it. And she lets me keep all the tip money from the tourists. I use it to buy comics and gifts for Gramma Carol on Christmas and her birthday. Now, it's time to show you one of Hoodoo House's first big secrets."

They went back into the house and ascended the stairs to the second floor. It was much brighter than the main level. The walls had all been given a coat of whitewash. Henry stopped at the first door he came to and opened it. It seemed to be an unimpressive broom closet.

"I think you'll like this," he said.

Henry pushed on a section of the wall near the back of the closet and it swung inward on hinges which groaned from disuse. Beyond the door was a square room less than four metres across. Bright light flooded down from above. Running along one side wall was a wooden staircase.

"Come on," Henry said. "It's a bit rickety, but it's safe."

Charlie stepped on the stairs. They creaked and shifted beneath his feet, and he reached for the handrail.

Henry smiled reassuringly. "I've been up it countless times and it hasn't collapsed yet."

"Great," Charlie said, trying to ignore the flutter in his stomach.

The stairs wound their way up the walls of the tall room, the height of which became more apparent as they climbed. And the more they climbed, the more Charlie became aware of how unsafe the stairs felt. After the third flight, the stairs ended on a more solid catwalk that ran around the perimeter of the tower.

"Welcome to the lookout," Henry said, arms opened wide.

Most of the windows were cracked, and several panes were missing. From the debris on the floor far below, Charlie could tell that birds had obviously roosted here.

"You can almost see forever," Henry said, staring out into the distance. "Sometimes I pretend this is my secret lair. I keep my eyes peeled for villains that I might have to smite."

Charlie looked out on the vista below him. There were rolling fields alternating green and brown, and deep coulees which slashed their way through the terrain. As he stared out through the window, he saw a hawk circling.

Henry pointed to it. "That's a ferruginous hawk. It's one of the great soaring birds in the area. It rides the updrafts, keeping its eyes peeled for ground squirrels and gophers to pounce on and eat."

After a few seconds of silence, Henry turned to Charlie. "This is my favourite part of the house. It doesn't feel like it was designed to depress the living hell out of you."

"Yeah, I see what you mean," Charlie said as he took a number of pictures, not because they would help the investigation, but because it was beautiful. He also carefully looked around the inside of the tower. This would be an interesting place to hide something, but there was no sign of a laptop anywhere.

Henry said, "Come on, I've got more to show you."

He led Charlie down the stairs, and back into the

broom closet, then made his way to the hallway of the second floor. Doors opened on both sides. Most of the rooms were either empty or were furnished with an old dresser, a chair and an unmade bed. While some had old framed pictures on the walls, none of them looked like they had been occupied in years. The one thing they all had in common, other than the ubiquitous flat white-painted walls, was the fact that they were spotlessly clean. Charlie photographed each, making audio notes about the numbers of each room—even room number six where Henry said the young prostitute had died.

Henry continued the tour. "And this is where I stay." The room showed an attempt at being tidy without much success. Some clothes had been roughly folded and placed on the chair. On the dresser was a brush which held some brown hair, and on the mirror above the dresser was an old photograph of three women in their early twenties smiling at the camera. There were also drawings taped up on the dresser mirror.

Charlie said, "So where did Mr Tull stay?"

Henry said, "I can show you his bedroom. It's just down here."

He led the way to a large room with a view out of the back of the house overlooking the deep, snaking coulee. The room smelled stale, like the bedroom of a single man not too focused on his own hygiene who never opened a window.

"Would it be okay if I took a quick look around?" Charlie asked. "I promise that I won't take anything. I'm just trying to get a better sense of the man."

"Sure. The police have already gone through everything. I did too...just in case the police missed anything, but I didn't find the computer you're after."

Charlie said, "You're a young detective in the making."

He perused the room, and took a few pictures. There was nothing particularly remarkable about it except that the room lacked any personal touch. He wrapped up his cursory inspection. It was like Tull had been no more than an overnight guest.

"What's next?" Charlie asked.

"There's one more thing I want to show you. I've been saving it for the very end. But it's something I think we need the detective's help to figure out."

Chapter Twelve

Declan took a sip of his tea. "The Harley you saw the day before Malcolm Tull died—did you recognize it?"

Mrs Cameron stared at the mug in her hand. "Mr Tull seemed to like men who rode motorcycles, but I couldn't say for certain if it was a bike that had been here before."

Before Declan could ask any more questions Henry burst into the kitchen, followed by Charlie.

"Declan," the boy yelled out. "There's something I need to show you and it can't wait any longer. I think it might be important to your case."

Mrs Cameron scowled. "Henry, you're interrupting our conversation."

"No. This is important. I've been patient, but I can't wait anymore. I might have an idea where the missing computer is."

Declan saw Charlie's eyes widen with surprise. Obviously this was news to him.

Henry took off, scooting past Charlie and back down the hall. He stopped at a door on the left side of the hallway.

"Come on!" Henry shouted.

By the time Declan, Charlie and Mrs Cameron had reached the hallway, they found a partly opened door and heard footsteps running down a set of stairs.

"I have a hunch I know what he's going to show you. It's part of the history of the house." Mrs Cameron said.

The three of them followed the sound down the old wooden stairs to a shelf-lined room. Henry was waiting in the far corner.

"This way," he said before he disappeared into thin air.

"What the...?" Declan said, looking to Charlie who stood beside him.

Mrs Cameron shook her head. "It's a trick. You'll see in a moment."

"Come on!" Henry called out from...somewhere.

Declan walked to the corner where Henry had last been seen and discovered the gap behind the shelves. While Henry could run the short length of the gap, Declan had to squeeze his muscled body through. When he made it to the end of the short passage, he let out a low whistle as he saw the opening of the tunnel.

Mrs Cameron crept in behind Declan, followed by Charlie.

"This must be the emergency exit Henry told me about," Charlie said. "It was a way for the bootleggers to avoid the police, wasn't it, Mrs Cameron?"

She nodded her head. "I don't know what the boy is going on about. There's nothing down here but dust and cobwebs."

Henry shouted out from ahead, "It's here! Quick, come here!"

They all felt their way along the tunnel wall, lit only by a dim glow of daylight somewhere in the distance.

Halfway along the wall, they reached Henry. Once everyone was beside him, he reached up to one of the battens that fixed the wall panels in place. He pulled on the edge of it and it pivoted out, revealing—

"A keypad?" Declan said.

"A *fairly new* keypad," Charlie added.

"I think it's a secret door," Henry said. "You can see where there are faint lines on the wall."

Mrs Cameron's eyebrows shot up in surprise.

"What's behind it? Any idea?" Declan asked Henry.

The boy just shook his head. "I've tried a whole mess of numbers, but none of them work."

Declan turned to Mrs Cameron. "Did you have any idea this was here?"

"This is the first time I've seen it. I knew about the passageway, but I don't tend to come down to the basement. I don't like spiders. Henry, how long have you known about this?"

Henry furrowed his brow. "I heard voices and a strange sound here on the afternoon before Mr Tull died. But then I thought I heard a scream and I got scared. I was worried maybe it was the ghost. And then when Mr Yamada phoned yesterday and said that the detective was looking for something, I thought I would do my own investigation and I came back here. That's when I discovered the loose board and the keypad."

Charlie examined the buttons on the panel. "There's no way to be sure how many digits there are in the code on this panel."

"Can you look at the surface of the keys to see which are dirtiest?" Declan asked. "That would at least limit the number of combinations of numbers used."

"Not with this type. Watch."

Charlie tapped one button and the LED digits on the

keys lit up. He let them go dark then tapped the same key again. This time the digits on the buttons were in a different order.

"Every time you touch the keypad, the order of the numbers changes. It makes it trickier for anybody watching you from a distance to remember the entry code."

"You're strong," Henry said to Declan. "Maybe you could just break the door down."

"I have no idea how thick this door is, and if it opens outward, I'd just break my shoulder trying," Declan replied.

"I think I know a guy who could crack the code on this," Charlie said to Declan. "He dropped out of my class in second year. He thought he could make a good living…freelancing in the security business, I think he called it."

"Is he like a bank robber?" Henry said, his eyes wide.

Charlie sputtered, "No, no. Not a *bank* robber."

"Call him," Declan said. "I think this mystery will have to wait until tomorrow."

Henry smiled and said, "I knew this was important."

Mrs Cameron ruffled his hair. "You've done well Henry."

Charlie looked down towards the slits of light at the far end of the tunnel. "What's down there?"

Mrs Cameron said, "It's the exit to the tunnel. Just a door made of slats really. We keep it secured but sometimes snakes and mice sneak in between the gaps. To my knowledge, it hasn't been used for a long time."

Declan saw Henry look towards the floor and suspected the door might have been used more recently than Mrs Cameron knew.

Declan walked to the end of the tunnel and examined the slats. The door opened inward, and was held closed by a board which anchored into two metal brackets on the inside of the frame. It looked like the dirt beneath the slats had been disturbed recently, but how recently was hard to tell.

"Henry. Have you been through this door lately?"

Henry shrugged. "Not for a while."

Declan leaned down and stared Henry in the eyes. "This is important. Have you been through this door since Mr Tull's body was discovered?"

Henry stared directly into his eyes and said, "No. I haven't been out this door in over three weeks."

Declan knew he was telling the truth.

Declan finished his inspection of the door then pivoted back towards Henry and shook his hand. "Henry, you've been a big help. Now do you have anything else you'd like to tell us?"

Henry grinned and said, "Nope. That's it. Are you coming back again?"

Charlie said, "I'm pretty sure we'll be back tomorrow."

They made their way up to the main hall and out through the front door.

Declan turned. "Thank you for your hospitality, Mrs Cameron. This has been very helpful. We'll call and let you know when we're returning with my friend."

"I'd much appreciate it," she replied.

Declan and Charlie made their way to their car. Before they could get in, Henry had bounded over to take a closer look at the Beast. "I'm glad I helped you. Just like the detectives in my comic books."

Declan grinned at him as Charlie took out his wallet, pulled out a business card and handed it to the teen.

"You know Henry, if you make any other discoveries that you think can help with the case, you can always reach us here. My phone number and email are on that card."

Henry studied it closely then looked at Charlie and said, "Cool. Thanks."

"No problem. And thanks for the tour of the house," Charlie added.

Henry cleared his throat. He was holding out his hand. "That'll be five dollars please," he said softly. "That's the going rate for the tour."

Charlie reached into his wallet. "I only have a ten."

"That'll do just fine," Henry said as he pocketed the bill, then he looked at the Beast. "That is such a cool car! Hey, can I have a ride in it sometime?"

"Sure," Charlie said, then leaned in close to him. "It'll only cost ya ten bucks."

Mrs Cameron waved to Henry from the porch. "Get over here and stop bothering them. It's time to do your English lesson."

Henry obliged and ran back to the house while Charlie and Declan got in the car.

As they were about to pull away, Declan spotted a man straddling a motorcycle just along the main road. He was looking at the house. Declan didn't think he appeared to be the type who would be interested in historic buildings, weird rock sculptures or romance writers. The biker sat on his Harley. He wore an old-style helmet on his head—a brain bucket—and was dressed in full leathers. He had a long scruffy beard and his eyes were covered by steampunk goggles. He scanned the property from the concession road.

"Now, what the hell do you suppose he's doing here?" Declan asked.

Charlie pulled out his phone and snapped a quick picture.

Declan stepped out of the car so the biker knew he was being watched. The biker fired up his engine and drove off.

"Should we follow him?" Charlie asked.

"Not sure," he said, keeping an eye on the bike. "Let's let it be for now."

They drove for a few minutes before Declan said, "Did Henry say anything else that might be of interest?"

Charlie flipped through the pictures on his phone. "He and Tull didn't get along, but that seems to be a theme." Charlie came across the pictures he had taken from the turret. "Oh, I almost forgot, Henry also showed me a secret door that leads from the second floor to the observation tower."

"A secret door?"

"Yup," Charlie replied. "Hidden in the back of a broom closet. No computer. I checked."

"That truly is a house of mystery."

"How about you?" Charlie asked. "Did you get anything out of Mrs Cameron?"

"Well," Declan started, "Sinclair Yamada had an all-out screaming match with Tull the evening before he died."

Charlie frowned. "We knew Tull was blackmailing him, but I don't recall him mentioning an argument."

Declan said, "I think we need to set up another meeting with Mr Yamada. See if he's available to see us at the office tomorrow. There's something bigger going on here, and I don't think he's telling us the whole truth."

Charlie's stomach moaned. "Are you hungry? I could use a bite."

Declan nodded. "Let's head into Rosebud. There must be a place to eat there."

He turned at a sign indicating '*Rosebud 3 km'*.

"You and the kid seemed to be getting along well," Declan said.

"He scammed me out of ten bucks."

"With a kid like that, I think you got off easy."

Charlie nodded. "I suspect you're right. I also gave him our business card in case he figures his way through that keypad. Somehow I think he's gonna get there before we do."

"Well, we'll have to talk to him again regardless," Declan said. "I want to see if he knows anything more about the door in that tunnel that leads outside. I didn't say anything, but I think it's been used recently."

* * * *

Charlie was in a much better mood than during the drive out. When he was focused on work, he and Declan clicked. For now, that was where he had to focus his attention. He got on his phone and called Sinclair Yamada. The call went straight to voicemail. Charlie checked his calendar and left a message asking Sinclair to come into the office around one the following afternoon. Then Charlie called the office number and discovered there were three messages, all of them from Cody White.

Charlie turned to Declan and said, "Cody White sounds desperate. He said he's in deep trouble."

"Call him, and set up an appointment for tomorrow, after Sinclair's meeting," Declan replied.

Charlie called Cody White's number, but it went straight to voicemail. Charlie left the details of the office location and suggested a meeting time of three p.m.

Just as he finished his call, a loud squealing sound came out of the engine compartment. The smell of burning rubber came through the vents and steam began to waft up from beneath the hood. The needles on the temperature and alternator gauges began to skew upward.

"Crap," Declan muttered.

Charlie remained silent.

Declan pulled to the side of the road. He got out of the car and popped the hood. Charlie joined him. The problem became immediately obvious. It was a broken fan belt.

"You're not wearing pantyhose, are you?" Declan asked Charlie.

"I didn't think it was that kind of car trip."

"It's an old remedy for a broken fan belt. I don't think the Beast is going anywhere tonight. Do you have an emergency kit in the trunk?"

Charlie nodded. "Yup, but not one with a fan belt, if that's what you're thinking. Let's see what else I've got back there."

Charlie opened the kit and found little of use, but was able to set up warning reflectors behind the car. It was decided they would head on foot for Rosebud. Declan assumed it would be faster to get a local mechanic to do the work than calling CAA. After all, by his estimation, they were now less than a kilometre from town.

Chapter Thirteen

It was thirty minutes later when Declan and Charlie found the Rosebud Inn, a large two-storey clapboard house. Unlike Hoodoo House, it was covered in a fresh coat of white paint. They climbed the three steps to the light grey wooden porch which wrapped around three sides of the building. The porch roof was supported by slender turned posts that were covered with machine-carved decorations, each painted in alternating muted colours of maroon, blue and green. Declan thought it was a bit fussy, but complementary to the style of the architecture. On the porch were a number of white-painted wicker chairs with overstuffed cushions in floral prints. An elderly woman, also in a floral print, sat on one of the rocking chairs. She was so still that he didn't see her at first. In her lap was a pudgy sable-coloured ball of hair with heavily lidded eyes and a curly tongue. Declan nodded. The woman smiled and nodded back.

"My sweet Pekingese Frisky would say hello," she said, "but he's done in. Been chasing a ball all afternoon and he'll be out until happy hour."

"A very sensible dog," Charlie said.

"That he is," she said, scrubbing him a little too harshly on the head. The dog woke, and nipped at the woman's hand.

"And playful," she continued as she thoroughly fussed him up. The dog let out a yap, then settled back into her ample lap and seemed to fall asleep.

Declan and Charlie walked past her up to the front desk and rang the antique bell sitting on the counter. A sleepy-looking face popped up from behind the desk. It was attached to the body of a young man. He was about Charlie's age. His name tag identified him as William. He brushed himself off.

"Please don't tell anyone you found me napping behind the counter. The boss would not be too pleased with me."

"Your secret is safe with me," Declan said as he flashed him a big smile.

William smiled back. "Frisky usually naps with me and barks as soon as he hears someone coming up to the desk. I'm not sure where he is."

"I think you'll find him curled up in a woman's lap outside," Charlie offered.

"That would be Mrs Carlyle. She's been a resident here for the last few years, ever since her husband died when he was run over by his cow."

"Pardon?" Charlie said.

"I saw it happen. It took the cow a good two minutes from start of run to the ultimate collision. I yelled at him and waved my arms but old Mr Carlyle was short-sighted and deaf as a post and paid no attention to me. He turned around just before Concetta hit him. That heifer threw him a good ten feet. It was truly tragic."

"It certainly sounds like it was," Declan said, trying

to maintain his composure.

"Now how can I help you?" William asked.

"Well, for starters," Declan said, "our car's broken down just south of town on the highway. Is there a mechanic in the area?"

"That was Mr Carlyle," William said sadly.

Declan paused. "Is there anyone else in town?"

"Oh sure," William replied. "His son has the business now. I could give him a call to see if he could fix it, but I don't think he'll be able to look at the car until tomorrow."

"Why's that?" Charlie asked.

William lowered his voice to a whisper. "Well, his mother out front told me he went into Calgary. He's got a date, and I don't think he's gonna get back until the morning. But if you like, you could wait around in case the date goes badly. In the meantime, we have a fine restaurant if you're interested in dinner. And if he doesn't make it back, we also offer accommodation."

Declan shrugged. "What do you say, Charlie? Why don't we live large and spend the night?"

"Sure, why not?" Charlie replied.

William looked down at the register. "You're in luck. We have one room left. It's the Honeymoon Suite with a king-sized bed and a pullout couch in the living room…in case somebody snores."

"We'll take it," Declan replied.

William looked at them, tilting his head slightly to one side. "You two wouldn't happen to be on your honeymoon, would you?"

"No!" Charlie and Declan said together.

"Because if you were," William said carefully, "the hotel would provide you with a complimentary bottle of champagne at dinner in our county-famous dining room."

He looked at them, hopefully.

Declan glanced at Charlie then grinned. "Well, babe, what do you say?"

Charlie glowered at him.

Declan turned back to William and said, "We would be honoured to take you up on your offer."

William smiled. "Great. Oh, and just a heads-up. It's not real champagne, it's a sparkling wine...from the Okanagan Valley."

Charlie and Declan took the keys from William and walked up the stairs to their room. It was the lone room in the attic of the house. Declan unlocked the door and announced that he would take the bed and Charlie could have the pullout. Declan looked around the room. It really was quite pretty with a nice view over the farm fields, including a pasture with a single cow.

I wonder if that's Concetta?

"Shall we go down for dinner?" he asked.

Charlie nodded. "Sure."

"We'll put it on Sinclair's tab," Declan said as he headed towards the door.

Charlie paused. "Just gimme a sec. I'm going to text Carrie and let her know I won't be coming home tonight. I don't want her to worry."

He quickly tapped a message into his phone, then they made their way down to the dining room, just off of the lobby. It was small with six tables, five for two people, and a corner table for four. Sitting at the table nearest the fireplace was Mrs Carlyle. She was propped up on what appeared to be two phone books and a floral cushion. Frisky the Pekingese occupied the opposite chair.

As they tried to decide whether they should take a table or wait to be seated, Mrs Carlyle said, "Just grab any seat. Fergus will be in soon to take your order. I always have the steak tartare. That way if I can't eat it all, Mr Frisky will take care of it."

"He seems like the perfect date," Declan said with a wink.

They took the table by the window and waited for the waiter named Fergus.

After ten minutes of discussing the events of the day, they were interrupted by a "Good evening gentlemen. I understand we have a special occasion tonight."

They looked up to see William, now dressed in a black suit and white shirt wearing a name tag that identified him as Fergus.

"William?" Declan said.

"It's Fergus, sir," he said, pointing to his name tag. "Management doesn't like people to think they can't afford to hire another staff member," he whispered.

"Well then, Fergus," Declan said. "Yes, my… husband and I are celebrating our honeymoon."

"Well, congratulations. Management would be pleased to offer you a complimentary bottle of our finest sparkling wine." Fergus, née William, leaned in close again. "I've just been told we can't call it champagne anymore. Something about trademarks."

"I understand," Declan whispered back.

Fergus the waiter nodded and scampered off.

"Well, *husband*, it looks like we managed to save Sinclair some money on the wine," Charlie said.

"It will make up for how much we're going to spend on dinner," Declan replied. "Have you looked at the menu?"

Fergus returned, crestfallen. "I regret to inform you that the hotel is out of the Okanagan's finest sparkling wine. Can I offer you something else?"

After a quick look at the menu, they opted for a couple of glasses of an expensive pinot noir, followed by the filet mignon, medium rare, with garlic mashed potatoes and asparagus.

Once they had finished their meal, they made their way back up to the room. After they'd reached the suite, Declan turned to Charlie and asked, "Up for an after-dinner drink?"

"I wouldn't say no to more of the pinot."

"My thought exactly. Be right back."

It took Declan ten minutes to locate Fergus and procure a few more glasses of wine. When he returned, he found Charlie sitting on the floor in front of the bookcase.

"I've been doing some research since you've been gone," Charlie said, holding up a copy of *The Ragtag Crew*.

"I've done you one better," Declan said, holding up a DVD of the movie. "This'll save us time."

Declan and Charlie discovered that there was no DVD player hooked up to the television in the living room, but there was one in the bedroom. And the TV was larger there so, glasses of wine in hand, they climbed onto the king-sized bed to watch the celebrated adaptation of Marjorie Ellis' vaunted novel.

* * * *

Declan woke up to a blue-screened TV. He must have fallen asleep during the movie. He couldn't figure out how something that had won so many awards and accolades could be so boring. Even his arm had fallen asleep.

It was at that moment that he realized why his arm was tingling. Snuggled into him, head resting on his shoulder, hand on his chest, knee over his leg, was Charlie. Declan's arm was wrapped around him. Charlie had fallen asleep practically on top of him and Declan had to admit, he loved it. Charlie's head, with its unruly mop of blond hair was within easy kissing distance. He leaned his head closer to it and breathed in his scent.

What would Michael think about this?

He lay there for a few minutes before sliding his arm out from under Charlie's head and letting it settle on the pillow. He moved Charlie's hand off of his chest and ever-so-gently slid Charlie's knee off of his leg. He removed himself from the bed, his bed, and stood, looking at the man he found himself married to, if only as a joke to get a free bottle of wine. He sighed. Why couldn't things be different with Charlie?

Declan couldn't resist. He bent down and gently kissed Charlie on the head, a mere caress of his hair with his lips, then turned off the TV and the bedside lamp and went out to the living room to sleep on the couch.

Chapter Fourteen

Henry walked into his bedroom and closed the door behind him.

When he had arrived four years ago, Mrs Cameron had shown him around the house and let him pick which bedroom he wanted for his own. There were plenty to choose from but he had chosen the last room at the end of the hall. It was the perfect size. Not too big. And it had a twin-sized bed like the one at his Gramma Rachael's house, and a dresser just like the one he used to have there.

He got down on his hands and knees and reached under the bed. From the space between the top of the box spring and the wooden slats that formed the bottom, above the old fabric which used to seal it in, he pulled out an old cigar box. He gently placed it on the bed.

Henry carefully opened it up and, one by one, removed the items from inside. There was a small ceramic bird that Gramma Rachael had given him. There was a puzzle that Gramma Carol had made for him as a part of a math test. She was really smart when it came to things like puzzles. He had wanted to keep this one because it was particularly tricky and he had solved it by himself. At the bottom of the shallow box, protected in a brown paper envelope, was an old photograph. It was a picture of a young woman. It was all that he had to remind him of his mother.

Each night he would take it out of the box and he'd tell his mother what had happened that day. He knew it was probably silly, but he'd hoped that somehow she would hear what he said and she wouldn't worry about him.

"Mom, you'll never believe it—I met a real detective this morning. Just like in my comic books. And I led him to a key piece of information that might help him solve the case he's working on. I know you would be proud of me.

"Anyway, I'm going to brush my teeth now and get ready for bed. I love you, Mom. I'll talk to you tomorrow."

He then kissed the photo, put it back into the envelope and stowed it away in the old cigar box which he tucked back under the bed. While he was down there, he knelt by the side of the bed, clasped his hands together and prayed.

"God bless Mom—please don't let her worry about me, and bless Gramma Carol for taking good care of me, and to Miss Ellis for making all things possible. And God, if you can, take care of Mr Tull, wherever he is. Oh yeah, and God, please forgive me for any stupid things I did."

* * * *

Malcolm Tull stood at the foot of her bed, dressed like a ghost from Charles Dickens' A Christmas Carol. *He pointed a finger at her and said through clenched teeth, "This is all your fault. I will make you pay…"*

Mrs Cameron woke with a start then made her second trip to the bathroom that night. It wasn't unusual, but that didn't make it any less annoying. She couldn't remember the last time she'd slept through the night. Mrs Cameron threw on the robe which was draped over her bedside chair, slid on her bedroom slippers and made her way to her bathroom across the hall.

The facilities hadn't been there originally. Thomas Pritchard had made the case to the Heart's Shadow Foundation board when she came to work for him after he started his residency. She remembered him exclaiming over the phone, "*It is wrong for a woman of her status to find herself in the position of climbing that Himalayan flight of stairs in the dark of night. Surely she deserves the dignity of more than a pail to piss in? Where is your humanity?*" The two had had a great chuckle about that over a few glasses of sherry. His reminder to the foundation later that it could be deemed a workplace safety issue that could cost them a bundle if she were to trip and fall had put the nail in the coffin of her nightly sojourns up the stairs. The renovations were made, providing her with her own main-floor washroom transformed out of an unused storage room.

As Mrs Cameron made her way back to her room, she felt a slight breeze coming from the direction of the front door.

Henry!

It was one of the boy's chores to check that all of the doors and windows were firmly secured before he went to bed. Two years ago, a rabid fan of Marjorie Ellis had snuck in through an open window and was discovered early in the morning sitting at the desk in the writer's room.

Mrs Cameron made her way to the end of the hall and secured the latch. It was a tricky door to lock as it had warped over the years and she had to throw her full weight behind it to allow the latch to catch. She had to give the boy a little leeway. He weighed almost nothing.

As she turned back towards her room, she noticed the writing room door was slightly ajar. She thought it had been closed before she had retired for the evening but maybe she was misremembering.

Mrs Cameron wasn't easily spooked, but after her dream, she wasn't taking any chances. She hurried back to her room and locked the door. She'd been facing up to too many ghosts lately and wasn't about to go hunting for another.

* * * *

Henry hadn't slept well, which was odd. He usually slept through the night. He kept waking up, thinking he was hearing sounds. He looked at his clock. It was 5:47 in the morning.

He swung his legs over the side of the bed and slipped on his bedroom slippers, then shuffled over to the door where his robe hung on a hook. He managed to get it on after a few tries, finally getting the left arm into the left sleeve and the inside of the robe on the inside. He scuffed his way across the hall to the bathroom. As he stood there peeing he thought, now that Mr Tull was gone, this was *Henry's* bathroom and Henry was peeing in *his* toilet. And there would be no threat of being yelled at for leaving splatter marks on the rim or for not sitting down to pee. He wiped the rim of the bowl down with a piece of toilet paper and flushed. Just because it was now his toilet, didn't mean he had to turn into a pig.

He slowly made his way downstairs and into the kitchen, making as little noise as possible. Gramma Carol rose early enough as it was without making it worse by getting her up any earlier. He took down the old percolator from the shelf, measured in the water and coffee and got it burbling away on the stove. He sat down and stared out through the window.

Is this what being old feels like?

He pictured himself in the future. Not thirteen, like he was, but old — like forty — living alone, not sleeping, sitting at his kitchen table waiting for his coffee to perk. He would be thinking about something adult, like…life insurance. Maybe Mr Tull was lucky to be dead. People should have best-before dates, like yoghurt.

What would mine be? he wondered.

"What are you doing up so early?"

He turned. Gramma Carol was at the door.

"Couldn't sleep," he said.

"Thinking about the problems of the world?" she asked.

"Pretty much."

He watched her as she glanced towards the percolator bubbling away.

"Coffee?"

"I thought it was time," he answered as he got up and took it off the heat and went to get a mug.

"How did you learn to make coffee?"

"I watched you," he replied.

"Hmm. Did you put a pinch of salt into it?"

"Yup."

"Hmm," she said as she settled into a chair at the table, the one facing the hallway. "Did you make enough for me as well."

"Of course," he said, putting down the mug in front of her. "I made a full pot. Here you go. Milk, one sugar, isn't it?"

"You do pay attention."

Henry returned with a mug for himself, half coffee, half milk.

"You know, at your age you shouldn't drink too much of that," she gently admonished.

He nodded and took a sip from his mug.

They sat in silence for a few minutes. Henry stared out through the window, and Gramma Carol stared down the hall towards the front door.

"You look tired. Up reading late last night?" she asked.

He nodded. "I noticed something funny in the last issue of my comic book. Something wasn't right, so I went back to the start and read all of them again."

"All of them?" she asked.

He drained the rest of his mug in a single go.

"In the latest issue, the writers said that Marty Finn's mother was a secretary. I was sure that she was a cleaning lady. I checked and I was right. As usual."

Gramma Carol raised her eyebrows.

"Well then, Mister Right. Maybe you have an answer to this question. Did you lock the front door last night?"

"Yup."

"Are you sure? I know it can be a bit tricky."

Henry looked at her. "I find that if you put your left hand on that gouge in the door beside the window and put your weight behind it, you can close it enough that the lock'll catch."

"On the gouge beside the window…"

"Yup. That's the sweet spot," he said, smiling, getting up and moving towards the coffee pot.

"You go easy on that stuff. I don't want you getting all wound up."

Henry smiled softly. "I can handle it. Now why were you worried about the door?"

"Because I got up last night and it was open."

Henry frowned. "But I know I locked it."

"Maybe," she said, "your 'spot' isn't as sweet as you think. Hopefully nothing got in. If I find a prairie dog running loose in the house, you're going to be the one to deal with it."

"If I catch it, can I keep it?"

"No!"

"Aww," he said, pouring himself a second cup of coffee.

"And speaking of doors, the one to the writing room was also open. Were you in there last night?"

"No."

Gramma Carol wiped her hands on her apron, and headed down the hall. Henry followed close behind. She stood in front of the door to the writing room and opened it wide. Henry didn't see anything out of the ordinary, and clearly neither did Gramma Carol who breathed a sigh of relief and said, "Everything seems to be in order," then headed back to the kitchen.

Henry remained in the room. Something wasn't quite right. Henry focused. *The bookshelves*. Everything was neat and tidy but it looked somehow…different. He closed his eyes and pictured the room the way he last remembered it, then opened his eyes and compared what he saw. There was definitely something different about the books behind the writing desk, but what was it exactly that was bothering him? He shook his head in frustration, then he had an idea. He needed to call Charlie.

Chapter Fifteen

The sunlight filtered in around the edges of the blinds. Charlie was confused for a moment. His eyes still half shut, he reached around him. The bed seemed to have grown in the night. He realized that this was not his and Carrie's apartment. But where…?

The Rosebud Inn!

"Declan?"

Charlie took in his surroundings, then crept out of bed and poked his nose out into the living room. Declan was sound asleep on the couch. He hadn't even bothered to pull out the hide-a-bed. He'd just lain down on top, and was still fast asleep. He looked adorable.

Charlie crept back into the bedroom and closed the door. He might as well get some work done while he waited for Declan to wake. It was only a quarter past eight in the morning.

Charlie opened his notepad and reviewed his notes. Something was bothering him. He felt like he'd missed something. As he flipped through the pages of his book, there was a rustling sound in the other room, then a head jutted around the door.

"Good morning," Declan said.

"Good morning," Charlie replied with a smile.

Declan smiled back. "I'm just going to grab a hot shower. My neck has a wicked kink in it for some reason."

"You should have woken me up," Charlie said.

"Are you kidding? You were dead to the world. I couldn't have woken you if I'd tried. After I'm done, we'll go down for breakfast then see about the car."

"Sounds good," Charlie said.

Charlie heard the shower turn on and the curtain rings jingle as they were pulled across. He pictured Declan under the water, soaping up his body, imagining what it would feel like if they were his hands doing the work. Declan would turn around, letting the hot water pummel his back as his taut muscles relaxed. He pictured himself there with him, massaging those massive shoulders.

The water turned off and the shower curtain jingled open. He heard Declan pull the towel off the rack.

Charlie realized that the door to the washroom was still open a crack. He moved so that he could see inside, yet stood back far enough that Declan wouldn't see him. Declan was rubbing himself vigorously. His back was towards Charlie. Declan worked the towel down his muscle-corded back then towelled off his ass. Charlie found himself shaking, wanting to break into the room and touch everything. Did Michelangelo have that feeling towards his model as he sculpted David?

But then Charlie's thoughts returned to last night... and this morning. They'd been in the same bed, and nothing had happened. Maybe Declan wasn't interested anymore. Charlie had asked about Michael and Declan had avoided the conversation. He decided to move back to the couch and focus on his notes. He'd talk to Declan more about his feelings at a later time. Right now they had work to do.

When Declan had finished in the bathroom, they headed down to the front desk where they discovered William was on duty.

"Did you have a nice stay?" he asked.

"We certainly did," Declan replied.

Charlie noticed William was wearing his Fergus name tag. Charlie pointed to it. "You might want to change that."

"Oh no, sir. Fergus and William alternate duties daily."

"I see." Charlie said, although he wasn't really sure if he did. "Is breakfast being served in the dining room?"

"Yes sir. A complimentary breakfast buffet is included with your stay. Feel free to help yourself."

"Great," Declan said. "And I'll take care of the bill now."

As Declan paid, Charlie enquired, "Did Mrs Carlyle's son get back into town? We still need the car fixed."

Fergus-William smiled. "Yup. I contacted Jeb this morning. He'll swing by when you're ready and take you out to it. I'll let him know when you're done breakfast."

"Thank you...Fergus," Declan said.

They ate a quick breakfast, then had Fergus-William call Jeb Carlyle. He arrived in a tow truck that appeared to be from another era. It had a battered cable winch on the back attached to a swinging hook. The vehicle was covered in patches of rust, and didn't look suitable to tow anything. Charlie and Declan squeezed into the front seat and headed down the road to where they had abandoned the Beast.

Jeb got out first and swaggered up to the car.

"Beautiful piece of workmanship, these cars are," he said. "A 1970?"

"Yeah," said Charlie.

"Thought so. No better car came out of the US that year. Let's see if we can fix the problem."

He popped open the hood and in no time, had the broken fan belt replaced, then topped up the radiator with water for good measure.

"See if it'll start."

Declan got into the driver's seat. He turned the key in the ignition and the engine roared to life.

"Thank you for rescuing us, Mr Carlyle," Declan said. "How much do we owe you?"

"Let's see...twenty-seven bucks for the belt...Let's make it thirty-five. Cash, mind you. I can't take credit out here."

Declan smiled and gave him the cash.

Jeb took the money in hand, then got back into his tow truck and waved as he headed up the road towards Rosebud.

Charlie was just about to get into the car when his cell phone rang. He dug in his bag, fished out the phone and answered the call, "Charlie Watts speaking."

"Hey, Charlie, it's Henry."

"Hey, Henry, is everything okay?"

There was a slight pause before Henry continued. "Oh, we're good, but something strange happened last night. Do you think you could come back to Hoodoo House? I need to see the pictures you took of the writing room yesterday."

"As a matter of fact, Henry, we're just outside Rosebud right now. We can be there in a few minutes."

"Great," Henry said. "See you soon."

Declan gave Charlie a puzzled look.

Charlie hung up and sat in the passenger seat of the car. "That was Henry. He wants us to come back to Hoodoo House. Something about the pictures on my phone of the writing room."

"Well, no harm in going back since we're already here. Wanna drive?" Declan asked.

Charlie smiled. "I'm fine. I'm beginning to like the idea of being chauffeured around."

* * * *

Declan and Charlie pulled up to the house twenty minutes later. Before they could close the car door, Henry was running out to greet them.

"Hey, Declan. Charlie. Did you really stay in Rosebud? I heard that the breakfast at the hotel is all you can eat. Is that true?"

"Yeah. It is," Charlie answered.

"If it was me staying there, I'd still be eating! Hey, you guys are wearing the clothes you had on yesterday."

This kid doesn't miss a thing, Charlie thought.

"We weren't planning on staying. The car broke down," Charlie replied.

"Oh, no. I hope it's okay now," Henry said, gently rubbing the hood of the car.

"It's good as new," Charlie replied.

Declan started towards the house. "I'll go in and let Mrs Cameron know we're here."

"There's a pot of coffee on the stove," Henry shouted as Declan walked away.

Charlie turned towards Henry. "So, tell me. What happened last night?"

"I think someone was in the house. The front door was open, and the door to the writing room too. I think someone was in there looking around the books in the office, but I'm not sure why. I need to see the picture you took on your phone yesterday, the one of the bookcase. I can't quite figure it out, but something's different in there."

Charlie and Henry walked into the house and made their way into the writing room. Charlie called up the images of the bookshelves. He passed his phone to Henry. Charlie glanced at the picture then the bookcase. Everything seemed pretty much the same to him.

Henry stared at the picture on the phone for thirty seconds straight.

"What are you doing?" he asked Henry.

"I'm looking at the way the room looked when you took the picture and locking that in my brain," Henry said. "It's like one of those puzzles. The kind where you compare two nearly identical pictures and pick out the ten differences. I'm really good at those."

Henry now stared at the wall of books behind the bare desk.

"Yup. Just as I thought. Some of the books have been moved. Someone's been in here, and whoever did it was careful to put them back and make them look tidy, but some are in the wrong order. Like *The Keys to the Kingdom*," he said, running up to the bookcase and pulling a large book off of the shelf. "It's the one where Mr Tull hides the key to his desk."

Henry opened it to reveal a hollow where a key rested.

Henry took the key and unlocked the desk drawer. He examined the contents. "Nothing's been touched here. I know what's supposed to be here and nothing's changed."

Charlie shook his head in disbelief. He decided not to ask why Henry knew what was supposed to be in the desk, at least not now.

Henry identified other books that had been moved. Charlie wondered who else would know to look for something hidden in the books.

"Are there any other books that have secrets like the one with the key? Or did you ever notice any books that Mr Tull used a lot?" he asked Henry.

Henry closed his eyes and concentrated. "I don't know…wait a minute." Henry scanned the bookcase. "There. Where it always is. On the top shelf," he said, pointing at a book with a yellow paper dust jacket.

Charlie reached up and pulled the book off the shelf. It was *Etiquette* by Emily Post.

"I saw that on his desk a bunch of times. I always thought it was weird that a guy like Mr Tull would care about manners."

Charlie rifled through the pages to see if there was a hollowed-out section or maybe something written in the margins. But nothing appeared out of the ordinary. As he went to put the book back, a small loose sheet of paper fluttered to the ground. Charlie examined it more closely and saw what appeared to be a list. It included passwords for Gmail and Proton email accounts, Tull's banking information and a few passwords for random websites. One stood out as different from the rest. The password had been crossed out and changed more than once and had only four digits — 6429. Beside it was a single word — Playroom.

"Henry, you're a genius. I don't know what the intruder was looking for, but this may help us solve the case. Follow me."

Charlie led Henry to the kitchen where Mrs Cameron and Declan sat at the table with mugs of coffee.

"I think I have something here," Charlie said,

holding up the piece of paper. "It might be the code to the door in the tunnel."

Declan raised his eyebrows in surprise. "How did you —?"

"I'll tell you later," Charlie replied. "Come on, let's see if I'm right."

With Henry in the lead, Charlie, Declan and Mrs Cameron made their way down into the cellar, around the shelves and along the tunnel. They stood in front of the keypad.

"Would you care to do the honours?" Charlie said to Henry.

The boy beamed, then tapped the pad, bringing it to life. He carefully entered the four-digit code. There was a click.

Henry reached to push the door open, but Declan stopped him. "Better let me do that."

"But I found the code," Henry complained.

Declan shook his head. "I don't know what's in there, Henry. I don't want anything to happen to you. Let me check it out first, then, when I know it's safe, you can be the second one in. How's that sound?"

Charlie could tell that Henry was disappointed. He was Howard Carter being told he couldn't enter King Tut's tomb. Still, the boy stepped back.

Declan pressed on the door to open it enough that he could reach his hand in and swipe it up the inside of the wall. Charlie figured he was trying to find a light switch. The lights came on in the secret room and Declan edged the door open enough to stick his head in. He pulled his head back out and said to Charlie, "Looks harmless enough."

Declan opened the door wider and stepped in, then said, "Your security team says it's okay to come in." Henry entered, followed by the others.

Charlie scanned the room. There was some wooden framework with ropes attached. In one corner was a leather and chain swing that hung from the ceiling. In the other corner was a bed, and on the wall were various small whips, riding crops and other implements. The roof and walls had dark grey foam covered in small triangles. "The room is sound-proofed."

Henry said, "This is a strange playroom."

Mrs Cameron said, "Henry, perhaps you should go and do your homework."

"But—"

"No buts. Upstairs, now!"

Henry, crestfallen, did as he was told.

Charlie walked over to a shelving unit by the door. On the upper shelf, he saw something. "Bingo," he said.

"What did you find?" Declan asked.

Charlie stepped up on the lowest shelf to get a closer look and pointed to a cardboard box with a circular cutout about the size of a loonie. He lifted the box to reveal—

"It's a high-res video camera that would normally be hooked up to…"

He pulled at the cable attached to it. He worked his way along the shelf, never letting go of the cable. He traced it the full length of the shelving unit then down the far end where it disappeared through a hole in a metal cabinet. The cabinet's door was locked.

Charlie looked around and spied a sturdy metal rod laying on a counter. He wedged it in the hasp which secured the locked door. "May I?" he asked Mrs Cameron.

"Be my guest."

He wrenched on it until it pulled free from the cabinet door. Inside he found what he had been looking for—a laptop that most likely belonged to Malcolm Tull.

Chapter Sixteen

Charlie opened the computer but was unable to get past the login screen. He tried some of the letter and number combinations from the sheet of paper they had found in the writing room. Tull had obviously used a password familiar enough to him that he hadn't bothered to put it on the list he'd hidden away in Emily Post's book.

"We'll have to take it back to the office," Charlie said. "I can use some software I have there to figure out the pass code. I hope you don't mind, Mrs Cameron."

"Take it," she replied. "The less I know about what that man recorded on it, the better."

Declan said, "Did you know about this room?"

"I knew about the tunnel, and I heard a rumour once that there was a hidden room to stash bootlegged whisky, but I'll be truthful, I don't like it down in the damp and never really explored too far. And that keypad looks new. Mr Tull must have had it installed on a day when I was out visiting my sister. How he knew about the room down here is a mystery that only he can explain, and he's dead now."

Declan said, "The room looks like it might have been used for…"

"His visitors? I guess that might be. But truthfully, he usually met them in his office and I kept to the kitchen. I never saw him head down to the cellar with anyone, but I suppose they could have met at the back entrance to the tunnel. Had I known this was going on…" She shook with anger. "And with a young boy in the house, no less."

Declan probed, "Did he always have visitors to the house?"

Mrs Cameron shook her head. "No, it was only recently. Just when I thought I couldn't hate the man anymore."

Declan said, "Well, let's lock up the room and we won't trouble you any further."

They turned off the light, closed the door and made their way up from the cellar. Henry was waiting for them at the top of the stairs.

"I had hoped we might find you at the kitchen table doing your homework," Mrs Cameron said to him.

Henry ignored her and looked towards Charlie. "Did you find what you were looking for?"

Charlie smiled and held the laptop in the air. "Yup. And it's all thanks to you."

Henry's eyes lit up. "Can I see what's on it?"

"We have to take it back to the office to find out," Charlie said. Then he whispered, "I'll let you know if we find anything important."

Charlie winked at him. Henry winked back.

* * * *

Traffic was light and it only took an hour and a quarter to get back to the office. Charlie set the laptop up on his desk and got to work. Declan stood behind him, watching. Charlie pursed his lips. "How about I come and get you when I have something to show you?"

"Right," Declan said, patting him on the shoulder. "Don't drive the tech genius crazy by hovering. I'll be upstairs putting on a change of clothes if you need me." Declan disappeared into the office and up the stairs to his apartment.

Charlie sat at the laptop working his magic and in less than thirty minutes he was in. The desktop showed dozens of folders. Interestingly enough, the primary documents folder had nothing in it, which meant that, on an old machine like this, Malcolm Tull likely wasn't automatically uploading his files to the cloud. If that was true, it meant the files on the desktop were probably only accessible through the machine in Charlie's hands.

Charlie scanned the names and honed in on two folders that caught his eye. One was labelled 'Manuscript', and the other was labelled 'Videos'.

The 'Manuscript folder' contained a single file called *Untitled_ME*.

The 'Videos' folder held three files which were named *SmoothStud123*, *BurlyBiker27* and *Wordsmith105*.

As tempted as he was to look at them right away, Charlie thought Declan should be down there for the big reveal. He took the laptop into Declan's office and hooked it up to the large TV monitor, then popped up to the apartment above. Charlie tapped on the door. "We have something, and I think it's good."

Charlie led Declan down to the office and sat him in his office chair, then went to the computer and opened the manuscript file. The title page identified it as *Untitled by Marjorie Ellis.*

Charlie started to scroll through the document. Within the first few pages, he lost track of the number of obscenities and improbable sexual positions it contained.

"Is this why Marjorie Ellis was your mother's favourite author?" Declan said, with a sly grin on his face.

"If my mother saw this, I think she would have dropped from a heart attack after page one. I don't get it. Maybe he was writing a raunchy spoof of her work just to piss her off?"

"Let's see what Sinclair says when he comes in," Declan suggested.

"That'll be in" — Charlie checked the clock on the computer — "thirty minutes."

"Let's move on to the videos," Declan said.

Charlie opened the main folder.

"Okay," Declan said, "let's start with the one labelled *Wordsmith105.*"

Charlie opened the file. It had definitely been shot in Tull's playroom. A figure walked towards the bed and started to undress. He was only visible from the back. He looked tall and well-muscled. Charlie quietly inhaled when the figure peeled off his underwear, unveiling a perfect ass. The man slowly turned around. It was Sinclair.

"Well, you said he looked great in a Speedo, and now we know why," Declan said.

Charlie fast-forwarded through the video, stopping every few minutes to see if there was a clear shot of the person other than Sinclair in the room. Never once did Sinclair give the impression that he knew he was performing for the camera. He followed the instructions of an off-camera voice. It was a deep voice, sensual and controlling, often correcting Sinclair, having him repeat sexual acts like he was a teacher and Sinclair was his eager pupil. Some scenes were done zoomed in and included actions involving the other man. The quality of the image led Charlie to believe that the close-up shots were done digitally after the film was recorded, possibly to allow the identity of the person who filmed the scenes to be cropped out.

"I think we can assume that the other man is Tull, given the fact it was shot in his playroom," Charlie said.

"I gotta give Sinclair credit — for such an uptight guy he seems really into it."

"Yes," Charlie agreed, "but you can see why he wouldn't want this out in the open."

Charlie opened one of the other videos labelled *SmoothStud123*. The man in the video was leaner. He also acted as if he didn't know he was being filmed. Each video showed only one of the men fully while all that could be seen of the other participant was a hand or body part. Sometimes the man was penetrating the lead performer with fingers, hands or toys. In the second video, he was choking the man, a bit of erotic asphyxiation.

Declan said, "Before we go any further, can you copy all of this to your cloud server, just in case something happens to the computer? Not for our own kicks...I have a hunch these videos might be important and I don't want to risk losing them if we turn over the computer to Sinclair."

Charlie said, "So we're going to give Yamada the computer?"

"That's what he hired us for," Declan replied.

"But don't you think there's a lot more going on here? What's on this computer might impact other people. I mean, look at those videos."

"I'll tell you what," Declan said, "before we turn everything over, I'm going to ask Sinclair some hard questions and we'll see what my gut says."

Charlie nodded. He spent the next ten minutes uploading the files to a safe place where only he could access them.

"Other than these files, do we have anything else to work with?" Declan asked.

"Oh, it keeps getting better. Do you remember the password list we found in the book?"

"Yeah."

"One of the passwords was for a Proton account."

"I have no idea what that is," Declan confessed.

"It's a security-encoded email system. Luckily Tull didn't use his internet incognito browsing window, so his username, *BakuBondageBoy*, was saved by the computer. And it looks like he had been sending out some interesting emails."

"Oh?"

"*BakuBondageBoy* had demanded money from *BurlyBiker27*—I assume the same *BurlyBiker27* of the video-filename we haven't watched yet. The email indicated that if *BurlyBiker27* didn't pay up, *BakuBondageBoy* would release the videos to 'you know who'. As you can see, *BurlyBiker27* replied with a threat to kill him if he didn't give him the files."

"Kill him?" Declan said, his eyes widening. "The guy actually threatened to kill Tull?"

"Well, he threatened to kill *BakuBondageBoy*, who I am assuming was Tull."

"Was Tull blackmailing anyone else?"

"*SmoothStud123*. Same threats. Money or he would give the video to a prominent judge. No idea who that would be. *SmoothStud123* was almost in hysterics in his responses."

"Did *SmoothStud123* threaten to kill the black-mailer?" Declan asked.

Charlie shook his head. "No threats of violence. And then there's *Wordsmith105*, who we know from the video label is Sinclair. He was also in an email war with Tull."

"Tull wanted money?"

"No. It's just like Sinclair said. Tull wanted a book published, untouched. He demanded it be printed just as he wrote it, no changes. And if that wasn't done, he threatened to…what did he say? Oh, yeah 'I'll bring down the mountain on all of your heads'. I wonder what that means?"

The security alarm beeped from the street-level door, and Charlie checked his watch. It was one o'clock.

Declan smiled. "I guess we're about to find out."

Chapter Seventeen

Declan and Charlie stepped into the reception room. Sinclair Yamada stood by the office door.

"Sinclair. It's good to see you again." Declan walked up to him and shook his hand.

"Can I get you a coffee?" Charlie asked.

"No. That's okay. I got here early and had one at the café downstairs."

"Why don't we sit out here?" Declan suggested, indicating the couches across from Charlie's desk. "It's more comfortable than my office."

Sinclair sat down, then nervously asked, "What have you found? Did you get the computer?"

Declan said, "Before we get into that, I need to ask you a few questions. It appears that you haven't been completely honest with us, Sinclair."

Yamada scowled. "About what?"

"Well for starters, Mrs Cameron said that you argued with Malcolm Tull on the day before he died. Is there a reason you didn't tell us that?"

"I didn't think it was important. You already knew he was blackmailing me."

"Is that what you argued about?" Declan asked.

"Yes. As I told you, he had threatened to reveal the sex tape to my employer."

Declan stared Yamada down. "Anything else you'd like to share?"

"I can tell you he was in a mean mood, and he had clearly been drinking when we fought. What's this about?" Sinclair snapped.

Declan ignored the question and continued, "It seems that neither Tull nor his predecessor actually wrote much for your company. We were wondering why you would keep them on?"

Declan watched Sinclair carefully. He seemed uncomfortable with the question. He shifted a bit, removed his hands from his pockets then stuffed them back in again. He got up, walked over to the window and stared out at the street below.

"Have you discovered something that I don't know about?" Yamada asked.

Declan continued in a cool tone, "We found the computer. And it did have your sex video on it and also what appears to be the copy of the latest manuscript. You said Tull was writing a book, but there was something in the opening chapters that seemed familiar to Charlie here. At first he thought it might be a spoof of *The Heart's Shadow* series. Is there anything you'd like to tell us, Sinclair?"

Yamada turned his head to the side, then made his way back to the couch and collapsed into it. "Nobody was supposed to have access to the manuscript. You shouldn't have read it."

Charlie interjected, "Oh we didn't read much.

However, when I checked it against the other *Heart's Shadow* novels, the characters were the same. But this book...it was more like erotica."

"Well, I guess there's no getting around it. You need to know the truth."

"And that is?" Declan probed.

Sinclair glowered at him. "After Marjorie Ellis finished writing *The Offal House*, she had an...emotional upset, let's call it. I wasn't around of course. It was well before my time. She went totally off her rocker just before she finished the third book, *The Heart's Shadow*, which was to be the first in a series."

He shifted his gaze to his hands.

"So," he continued, "there was Mount Temple Press with an author who had a huge hit, a miss and a potential money-making series. Only apparently, she wasn't able to cope with the pressure. The solution was to bring in a ghostwriter to complete the task. That was Thomas Pritchard. This of course was after Marjorie Ellis had fled to Portugal. Thomas had been a correspondent of Miss Ellis'. When the publisher asked if she would be amenable to having someone else write under her name, she said that she had read his book, *The World Before Time*, and liked his writing. I don't know what she was thinking. It was his only book. Like I said, she was off her rocker. But she suggested he would be an acceptable replacement and against all odds, it turned out all right."

"So, she agreed to step aside and let someone take over her characters?" Declan asked.

"From what I was told, she knew she couldn't handle the stress of writing to the tight deadlines that were asked for. Her first book took ten years, the second, four. Mount Temple Press wanted a new novel at least once per year. She gave up complete control of the series and agreed to the setup of the foundation in exchange for a percentage of all future sales of books containing her characters. It worked in everyone's favour."

"So, Pritchard and Tull both wrote *The Heart's Shadow* novels?" Declan asked.

"Yes."

"And nobody knows they aren't written by Marjorie Ellis?"

"Maybe some have guessed, but officially, only myself, the publisher and the accountant who transfers the funds know. And to protect the brand, we have to keep it that way."

"Have you personally had communication with Marjorie Ellis since you took over as editor?" Charlie asked.

"No. Supposedly, the head of Mount Temple Press is in email contact with her, but I haven't personally had any contact with her. My job is to edit the work of the ghostwriter."

Declan stepped closer to him. "So, is she still alive?"

"Why would you say that? I mean, I couldn't say for sure, but I haven't heard anything to the contrary."

"Very interesting," Declan said.

Sinclair scowled. "I hope I can trust you not to reveal that you know the secret of the ghostwriters? After all, I came to you with the understanding that you would be discreet."

"Why is it so important that readers don't find out about the ghostwriters?" Charlie asked. "I mean, a lot of books are ghostwritten. V.C. Andrews' novels, for instance. They've been ghostwritten since she died."

Declan looked at Charlie who shrugged. "My mother reads a lot of romance."

Sinclair sighed. "For many of her fans, Marjorie Ellis is more than a writer. Her readers are rabidly faithful to her and many of them write to the publisher saying that they base their intimate fantasies on her characters through living in the world of her books."

"And what are you worried would happen if they found out that she no longer wrote the books?" Declan asked.

"They may feel tricked. Her works have been praised for accurately capturing the feelings and emotions of a predominantly female audience. One wonders what would happen if they found out they had been deceived by a male publishing team and male writers pretending to be her. If her image is tarnished, a takeover bid from a larger publishing house could collapse along with Mount Temple Press. The publishing industry is very delicate right now. I'd also likely lose my job and my head, and not necessarily in that order. You have to promise not to reveal what you have discovered."

Declan said, "We will keep your secret."

"Good," Sinclair said. "Now is there anything else?"

"Did Tull ever threaten to reveal the secret of the ghostwriters if you didn't let him get his way?"

Yamada shifted on the couch. "He intimated it."

"You mean with phrases like 'I'll bring down the mountain on all of your heads'?" Charlie asked. "I assume that *mountain* refers to Mount Temple Press."

A look of shock crossed Sinclair's face. "Yes. How did you know about that?"

"There is nothing Charlie can't find out," Declan said.

Sinclair scowled. "That correspondence was private and on a protected site."

Declan shrugged. "Like I said, Charlie's good at his job. Now, about the book Tull wanted to have published..."

"Malcolm wanted to put more erotic elements into the book. The readers would have abandoned the series entirely. But Tull was egotistical, single-minded and vindictive. He had me backed into a corner. He said that it was time *The Heart's Shadow* had more heat, and that the readers would just assume Marjorie Ellis had evolved."

"It doesn't sound like something Miss Ellis would have been in favour of. Did she read the manuscripts before they were published?"

"Never. Like I said, I was told she gave up control, in exchange for the royalties. As far as I know, her only involvement at this point is to take the money that is wired into her account."

Sinclair continued, "Revealing the secret of the ghostwriters was something Tull knew I could never allow, but he also knew I would do just about anything to stop him from revealing that sex video. That threat was like the extra topping on his masochist sundae. I was stuck in the middle of two unacceptable choices — my reputation or the continued life of the book series and my job."

"And now, conveniently, Malcolm Tull is dead, and we've found the computer with your missing sex video and the manuscript as well," Declan added.

"I didn't murder him, if that's what you're thinking."

Declan stared at Yamada, "Now why would you say that?"

"I'm just saying that there are many people who would have liked to see him dead, and the police said it was likely an accidental death."

Declan smiled. "Last time we spoke to you, you said it was currently ruled a suspicious death."

Sinclair paused. "So, where do we go from here?"

Declan said, "Technically, we should turn the computer over to the police, but I think given this conversation, we should hold onto it for a bit longer."

"And the sex video?" Sinclair asked.

Declan stared him down. "I want to make sure that I'm not erasing something that might be evidence connected to Malcolm Tull's potential murder. We're going to do a bit more investigating before we delete that video. You'll have to give us a little more time. If it turns out that Tull wasn't murdered, you can have the manuscript and your video."

Sinclair Yamada stood abruptly. "Why would I have hired you in the first place if I murdered Tull? That simply wouldn't make any sense."

Declan nodded. "Sometimes people think they can outsmart the system by being the one to get the ball rolling on the investigation. If you've told us the full truth, then you have nothing to worry about. Now, if you don't mind we have another appointment shortly. We'll be in touch."

Declan opened the door and a disgruntled Sinclair Yamada left the office, slamming the door behind him.

Chapter Eighteen

Mrs Cameron sat with a steaming hot coffee in front of her. She usually drank tea in the afternoon, but the boy had gone to all that trouble. He'd made a full pot earlier in the day and she had to admit it was a good cup of coffee. Henry set down a plate of buttered toast in front of her, along with a knife and a jar of her homemade Saskatoon berry jam.

"What's your game, mister?" she said with a sly grin.

"No game," he said, plopping a second plate of toast down in front of his seat at the table. "I just thought, since I'm getting older, I should start pulling my weight around here."

He dropped back into his chair grunting like an old man.

"Don't grow up too fast. I kinda like having a boy around," she said, reaching over and patting the back of his hand.

The phone rang. Henry jumped off his seat and quickly picked up the receiver. "Good afternoon.

Hoodoo House. Henry Quill speaking… Sure," he said, holding out the receiver to Mrs Cameron. "It's for you."

She looked at him quizzically and made her way to the phone. "Hello. Carol Cameron speaking."

"Mrs Cameron? Abigail Sweet from Red Deer Retirement Mansion here. Sorry to disrupt your day."

"What's she done now?" Mrs Cameron asked.

"The question really should be what has she *not* been doing?" Abigail replied.

Abigail Sweet never answered a question directly. She was like a bird that circled its prey before landing on it, talons at the ready. Mrs Cameron had had many dust-ups with this woman.

"Florence had a bit of a bad spell this morning. She nearly bit one of her caregivers—"

Do not kick her out. Dear God, do not let them kick her out…

"Then she became her old sweet self again. It's like someone flicked a switch! She pulled out the photo of the two of you and walked around the place showing it to everyone. I wish I had a sister who cared for me as much as Florence does for you. You are so lucky."

Get to the point, woman!

"Then, just after lunch…she's gone completely catatonic."

"Have you adjusted her medication? You know she doesn't react well if you do that," Mrs Cameron scolded.

"Nothing has been changed."

"Well, I guess you'll just have to keep your eye on her and see if her condition improves."

"Mrs Cameron, Red Deer Retirement Mansion is not set up to handle residents in your sister's present condition."

I'm surprised you wouldn't prefer all of them catatonic, rather than biting.

"If she doesn't improve, I'm afraid we'll have to transfer her to the Red Deer Regional Hospital, and she'll lose her spot here."

"Oh God, please don't do that," Mrs Cameron begged. "You know how long it took to get her in there!"

"I know your concerns and I'm fully behind you on that. I was thinking that if you could come in for a visit, maybe talk about old times, it could snap her out of it. Would you be able to do that?"

The wheels of Mrs Cameron's mind began to turn. Henry gave her a glance then whispered, "Is everything okay?"

She nodded then motioned for her coffee, which he ran to her. She took a swig.

"Mrs Cameron. Are you still there?"

"Yes, I'm still here," she said, trying not to sound annoyed. "I'm just figuring out what to do with my ward, here. He's thirteen and not used to being on his own."

"I can go with you!" Henry cried. She could hear the hope in his voice. He rarely got the opportunity to leave the property, but she would not expose him to Red Deer Retirement Mansion. Not Henry.

"I, um, guess I could leave him by himself for a while," Mrs Cameron said. "That's legal, isn't it? To leave a thirteen-year-old on his own? I mean I'll only be gone for the afternoon and into the early evening."

"I believe that's up to you to decide."

"I'll be okay by myself. I'll be fine. Honestly!" Henry said, dancing around.

"Well," Carol continued, "I'll have to prepare his dinner and arrange for a driver...I could be there around four. Yes. Five at the latest."

"That would be wonderful. I'll let Florence know. That might help to shake her out of her state."

"Well, in the meantime, keep an eye on her. I don't want her running away like the last time," Mrs Cameron snapped.

Miss Sweet hung up.

What a mess.

Mrs Cameron would have to press her best dress and do up her hair, although a hat covered many sins. Then there was Henry.

"When do you have to leave?" he said in excitement.

"Don't be so quick to kick me out of the door. Some day when I'm gone, you'll miss me all the time."

"Don't say that. Never say that," Henry said, running up to her and giving her a hug. She wasn't normally the hugging kind, but for Henry, she'd always make an exception.

"Don't worry. I'm not done teaching you everything you need to know just yet. Be a good boy and call Lem Franklin. Tell him I need a ride to Red Deer."

"Mr Franklin's a bit sweet on you, isn't he?"

"Now, what are you insinuating? That I would take advantage of Mr Franklin just because he may or may not harbour feelings for me?"

Henry grinned. "Nope. Just calling 'em as I sees 'em."

"And I'll be home later this evening, so you can occupy yourself with a bit of homework and maybe one of your puzzles."

"I'll be fine, Gramma Carol. I'm practically a grown man. I can take care of myself."

Henry ran over to the phone and arranged for her ride as she fussed in the kitchen, preparing a cold dinner and hoping that Henry would stay out of mischief while she was away.

It's only a few hours. What could possibly go wrong?

Chapter Nineteen

After Sinclair Yamada had left, Charlie pulled together notes on what he had gleaned during the interview then popped his head back into Declan's office.

"Cody White is scheduled to arrive at three. Is there anything I should prepare?"

Declan looked at his watch, then up towards Charlie. "I want you to handle Cody White on your own."

"What?"

"You're ready for it," Declan assured him.

"No, I'm not!"

"You are. In every single interview you've been involved in, you've instinctively known what to say and do to put the client at ease. And you're not physically imposing, so you don't threaten people."

"You're saying I'm good because I'm skinny?" Charlie asked.

"No. I'm saying you're good because you're *you* — likeable and approachable. You just have to find out what this guy wants. Get all the details of what he's willing to tell you, and we'll start with that."

"What if I miss something?"

"Then you miss it."

Declan gathered his phone from his desk and made his way towards the office door. "Charlie, this is only the first meeting. You don't have to solve the case tonight. I guarantee you'll never get everything out of a client. They forget. They get mixed up. They lie. It's our job to take all that, figure out what's important and what we still have to learn."

Charlie knew he should be excited, but something felt off. "So, while I'm talking to Cody out at my desk, you'll be in your office if I need something, right?"

Declan walked past Charlie. "No. I've got to meet up with someone."

"Does this have anything to do with Michael?"

Declan turned. "It's…unfinished business I've got to deal with. So, when Cody gets here, just treat it like it's a first date. Offer him a coffee and a snack, and smile a lot. Pick up a few of Gwen's pastries. I bet that and a nice cup of coffee'll help put him at ease. Anyway, I've gotta go. I'll text you when I'm done and see how it went."

Declan patted Charlie on the shoulder, then headed out of the office.

Charlie picked up one of the pillows on the couch, buried his head in it and screamed. Once he'd let out his frustration, he stood up, adjusted the pillows, and quickly exited down the stairs to Gwen's shop. He returned fifteen minutes later with enough pastries to feed a dozen clients.

Charlie set the pastries out on a platter on the coffee table in the reception room. He thought about how that would look — a bunch of snacks left over from an office function—so he took them into Declan's office—*his* office for now. Charlie might come across as pleasant and unimposing, but he was damned if he was going to come across as just the office boy.

He quickly worked out a game plan. He set out a notepad and pen on the spartan desktop, ready to jot down a few notes, so he'd look professional. He also set out his cell phone, which he would use to record the conversation just in case he needed to check the facts.

The alarm system beeped as someone entered the street-level door. Charlie pressed record on his phone and walked out to the reception area. The office door opened and in walked a good-looking young man. He wore a jean jacket, with the collar pulled up, and a baseball cap with the brim pulled down in front of his eyes which were obscured by a pair of aviator sunglasses. His hands were stuffed in the pockets of his perfectly worn jeans. He looked as if he'd stepped out of a contemporary film noir. A very sexy film noir. The man looked vaguely familiar. Charlie wondered if he might have seen him before at Bar-None.

"Cody White?" Charlie asked.

"Mr Hunt?" the man said uncertainly.

Charlie walked up to him and firmly shook his hand. "No, I'm Charlie Watts, Mr Hunt's…partner."

"I thought I'd be meeting with Declan Hunt this afternoon," Cody said, removing his sunglasses and looking at Charlie.

Don't lie! He'll know you're lying. Hot guys like him can sense it. They've been around. Now say something!

"My job this afternoon is to take down the details of your situation for Mr Hunt. He's out wrapping up another case at the moment. We've been very busy and he felt bad that you had to wait this long, so he wanted to get you in as soon as possible to see if we can help you."

"So you're the secretary?"

"Cody — is it all right if I call you Cody?"

"Sure."

"Cody, at Declan Hunt Investigations we work as a team — Declan, me *and* you. Once we get the details of your case, we'll be able to best assess how we can help you. Why don't you step into the office and grab a seat. Can I get you a coffee?"

"Sure. A latte if you've got it," Cody said.

Charlie nodded, went to the kitchenette and made Cody's drink. By the time he returned to the office, Cody had eaten three of Gwen's pastries and was looking slightly more at ease. Cody looked up sheepishly from the plate of desserts.

"I'm sorry I ate so much. I'm...a bit nervous. I've never had to hire a detective. I've never had something like this happen to me before."

Charlie smiled. "It's okay. There's nothing to worry about. Just tell me everything that's going on. I'll be taking notes, if that's all right with you."

Cody nodded. He appeared tired...and anxious. His fingernails were chewed. When he looked up, Charlie could clearly see his face under the office light. He had the most beautiful golden-brown eyes.

Charlie sat behind the desk and grabbed his notepad. "So how can we help you?"

Cody began, "I know that your firm deals with cases connected to the gay community. I need a place where I feel safe and I'm not going to be judged."

"I assure you," Charlie said, "whatever you say is in the strictest of confidence and we pride ourselves on serving our clients with their best interest at hand, without judgment."

Cody shifted in his seat. "I guess it's all pretty simple," he started. "I got together with a guy I met on an S&M internet hook-up site. Actually, we got together a few times. It was fun. He really seemed to know what he was doing…"

Cody went quiet. He stared into his lap.

"It's okay," Charlie reassured him.

Cody lifted his left hand and started chewing on his thumbnail.

"I haven't had a huge amount of experience with men. I'm just trying to figure myself out," he said, looking up to meet Charlie's gaze. "I wanted to live out one of my fantasies, and I thought this guy was into me—I thought we'd made a…you know, a special connection. But sometimes it took him a long time to return my calls and when he did, it seemed that he was only into the sex. God, I sound pathetic."

"No. Not at all."

We have a lot in common.

Charlie continued. "You sound like you're just figuring out your place in the world."

Cody nodded and settled back in his chair. He stopped nibbling at his nail long enough to take another sip of coffee. "This is really good. Thanks."

"You're welcome," Charlie said.

Cody's eyes started to well up. "It was after the last time we got together that he told me…he told me," Cody continued, "that he'd been recording our meetings—"

In a flash it came to Charlie. He knew who this was. It was *SmoothStud123* from one of the files on Malcolm Tull's computer.

Don't say anything. Let him do the talking.

" —and if I didn't give him a lot of money he would send copies of the files to one of his connections in the mob, and…" —he took a deep breath— "to my mother."

The last phrase he managed to choke out before breaking down into tears.

Charlie wanted to give Cody a hug, but he refrained. It would be unprofessional and he didn't want to blow this. He wanted to show Declan that he was worth more than Declan thought.

Charlie gently asked, "Does your mother know that you sleep with men?"

"I don't think she'd be surprised. Anyway, she has gay friends and has no problems with gay people. It's just that…"

Cody started to drum his hands on his thighs. "The sex in the video…it's a bit rough. Bondage, spanking, choking, that sort of stuff. Not what you want your mother to see. But what I'm really worried about is that he was going to send it to a guy in the mob and my mother's supposed to be trying a case in the next few months…"

"Is your mother a lawyer?"

"No. A judge. My mother is Associate Chief Justice Beverly White of the Alberta Court of Appeals. She's going to be trying the appeal of a case connected to a guy who is allegedly involved with a gang."

Charlie racked his brain. He'd read something about this case. It had to do with a crime syndicate. Then he remembered. The case had to do with the trial of a man who they had identified as being connected to—Charlie inhaled quickly—Monarch. He remembered his encounter with the thugs from Monarch only a few months ago, and they didn't play around.

"And how would the videos of you affect the case?" Charlie asked.

"I don't know. If the recordings came out, she might have to step down from the trial because of a possible conflict of interest. Not to mention what it would do to her reputation. I've fucked everything up, and all just to have sex with this guy."

"Okay, Cody. What's this man's name? The one blackmailing you."

"Malcolm Tull."

Charlie knew he couldn't disclose that they already had a connection to Cody's case, at least not yet. He had to continue the interview as if nothing was out of the ordinary.

"And where does he live?"

"A big run-down place outside of Rosebud. It's called Hoodoo House."

"Hoodoo House," Charlie repeated as he wrote it down. "And what is it that you want Declan Hunt Investigations to do for you connected to your situation?"

"I need you to figure out how to get a hold of those videos."

Charlie nodded. *Just play it cool. Don't give anything away, so you get the full story.*

"And have you had any contact with Mr Tull recently?"

Cody began chewing the nail on the thumb of his right hand. "I went to his place to beg him to give me the files. I don't have enough money to pay him off so I was going to offer myself up to him for whatever he wanted, but it was too late. When I got there, I found out he was dead." Cody looked at the edge of his thumb, which had begun to bleed, and stuck his hand in his pocket.

Charlie focused on his notepad. "So you didn't give Mr Tull any money?"

"No! I couldn't afford it."

"And your mother hasn't indicated that she has received the recordings yet?" Charlie pressed on.

"I'm pretty sure she would have said something," Cody replied.

Charlie leaned in. "Well, then why do you still think you need our help if Mr Tull is dead?"

Cody went still.

Charlie softened his tone. "Cody. This is important. You can trust me. Did you do anything to harm Mr Tull?"

"No! I swear it, but…what if the mob guy somehow got the tape before Tull died? What if they killed him for it? Tull gloated that he had it all on his computer. Look, I did something I shouldn't have. I just needed to be sure. After I found out he was dead, I broke into the house at night when everyone else was asleep to see if I could find his computer."

"Okay, Cody. When was this?" Charlie asked.

Cody pulled his left hand out of his pocket and began gnawing on the nail of his pinkie finger like a rat nibbling a piece of cheese.

"Last night. I snuck in through a back entrance. Tull showed me how to get in unnoticed."

Charlie focused intently, "And then what happened?"

Cody started nibbling on the next finger over. "I tried to get into his desk, but I needed to be quiet. There were other people in the house. So I needed to look in the books."

Charlie said, "What do you mean, you needed to look in the books?"

Cody stopped nibbling the fingers on one hand, and switched over to the other. "One day when I was meeting Tull, I got there early and looked in a window to see if he was there. I saw him take a key that fit his desk out of one of the books on the shelves. I figured maybe he'd hidden something in there, so I went back to find it. Maybe a USB key or his laptop."

"And did you find anything?" Charlie asked

"No. I couldn't remember which book it was in. I had a bunch of books pulled down and then I heard a noise. I panicked. So I quickly put them back on the shelf and went out of the front door."

Cody had run out of fingernails to chew on. "Look, I know it was a stupid thing to do, but I couldn't *not* take the chance."

Charlie nodded. "Cody, you've done the right thing to come to us. I just have one more question. Did anyone ever see you at the house when you came to visit Mr Tull?"

"The housekeeper and a kid that lives there. I'd driven by the property on my motorcycle before. On the day Tull died, I went to the house. The cops were just leaving, and the boy told me Tull was dead. I'm scared. I need to find out if the cops have the files, or the mob or...and if they don't, it would be great if somehow you could find them and make the files disappear."

Cody looked at Charlie with pleading eyes. "Can you help me?"

We already have.

Charlie knew he couldn't say anything until he talked to Declan.

"We will definitely take on your case. Let me talk to Mr Hunt and we'll be in touch shortly with next steps. We've dealt with other cases almost exactly like this, and I think we can help you."

Cody smiled weakly. "I'm counting on you."

He got up, put on his sunglasses, stuffed his well-chewed hands back into his pockets then left the office.

Charlie turned off the recording app on his phone, then texted Declan.

Need to talk as soon as possible. Cody White is involved with Tull

Charlie paused before he typed the next words.

…and Monarch.

Chapter Twenty

It was three-thirty when Mrs Cameron made her way through the front door. Henry waved as Mr Franklin's 1959 Cadillac Coupe de Ville with its enormous fins pulled out of the drive and headed onto the road towards the Red Deer Retirement Mansion.

Henry took a deep breath and headed back into the house, shutting the door behind him. He shoved it with all his might, making sure it was closed — and locked. Gramma Carol had made him promise. After all, it appeared someone had been in the house the other night. Henry had also promised he'd do his homework. Out of thin air, Gramma Carol had pulled the assignment — an essay of his choosing on the topic of Marjorie Ellis' *The Ragtag Crew*. He wandered into the writing room, plunked himself down on the chair behind the desk and swivelled back and forth. He spun harder until he felt dizzy. When he stopped, he was facing the bookcase. Right there, at eye level, was a copy of *The Ragtag Crew*.

He remembered being told that it was a first edition,

which meant it was in the first batch of books to be printed. People paid a lot for first editions, especially if they'd been signed by the author. He reached over and took the volume off the shelf. Inside, on the title page he saw it—the neat and tidy signature of Marjorie Ellis.

He held the book in his hand and flipped to the first page. He started to read the first line.

They were friends, not for reasons of love or admiration, but by —

"Boring," he called out. Then he noticed a note written in the margin of the page. It was referring to the comma before the word 'but'. The note read,

I distinctly recall using a semicolon here.

It was written in the same tidy handwriting as the signature. Marjorie Ellis had gone back and corrected the book. There were a number of these corrections throughout. At that moment, Henry knew what the topic of his essay would be—Editors Changing the Author's Mind. And he had the perfect reference material for this—the first edition and the sacred manuscript which was on the next shelf over. He picked them up and headed to his bedroom.

Henry thought about doing his homework, then it hit him. He realized that this was a milestone moment. For the very first time in the thirteen-year-old life of Henry Quill, he was alone. Truly alone. Not *going to the toilet* or *having a bath* alone. This was *real* alone. He felt like a bird flying out of the nest for the first time. He was technically still in the nest, but right now, at this moment, it was *his* nest.

Henry had the urge to do everything he'd ever thought of in the short time he had. Gramma Carol had planned on arriving in Red Deer no later than five, visiting with her sister for a few hours, which would make it seven, and arriving back to Hoodoo House by nine — ten at the latest she had said. That would give Henry at least five hours of freedom!

Henry went back down to the kitchen. He decided his snack would become an early dinner. When he opened the fridge, he discovered that Gramma Carol had made him a ham and cheese sandwich with a side of fresh-cut vegetables and an instant pudding for dessert. He pulled them out of the refrigerator. The cold air fell from the fridge and wrapped itself around him. He'd never felt cold air like this on his body before, but then again he'd never stood in front of the open fridge door naked before. Well, he wasn't truly naked — he still wore his underwear. Being in the kitchen completely naked…well, that just didn't seem right. He marched back to the table with his sandwich, and sat down at the head of the table. This was a day for breaking rules.

Next on the list — another cup of coffee, black. Grown-ups did it and he figured he'd have to start sometime.

Henry felt powerful, like a superhero in one of his comic books. Superheroes went on quests and adventures.

Henry was struck by an idea. He made his way down the cellar stairs, behind the shelves and along the tunnel. In a matter of seconds, he had located the vertical board he was looking for and punched in the code on the keypad behind it. Henry heard the click of a door latch opening. He pushed on the secret door and once it had swung open, he felt along the wall and flicked on a switch. The room was flooded with light.

In his head, he tried to figure out what was above him. He closed his eyes and his brain plotted out the route he took to get here. He soon realized that this room was directly below the old hotel's dining room, now Henry's puzzle room.

He looked around. The room was exactly as it had been before, but this time he decided he might look to see if there was anything that the detectives might have missed.

His coffee-fuelled brain didn't see anything of great use, but he did spot something of interest in the corner. On one of the tables was a black mask and it looked new. He tried it on. It was like the knitted balaclavas he had worn in the winter, but this was made of leather. It looked a little large, but when he did up the zipper it seemed to fit all right.

Now Henry was like a real superhero, but he was missing something. He looked around and discovered a shiny rubber baton. It was a bit heavy, like it was filled with sand, but it was perfect — a way for the superhero to protect himself. Henry took the mask and the baton, turned out the light then carefully closed the door and restored the panel to its original position. As Henry headed back upstairs to his bedroom, another idea crossed his mind. But not just any idea — a *fantastic* one.

He rummaged through his dresser and pulled out a pair of black jeans and a black sweatshirt which he put on. Then he donned the leather mask. Baton in hand, held out to his side, he looked at himself in the mirror. He couldn't believe it. What stared back at him was not the wimpy Henry Quill. It was The Slithe! He screamed with delight as he jumped around the room, doing his best impression of a martial arts expert. Today was the best day in Henry Quill's life.

Chapter Twenty-One

Declan stopped by the local flower shop and bought a bouquet of tiger lilies. He checked his watch — three-forty-five, fifteen minutes to go.

As he parked his van and walked up to 16th Avenue and Centre Street, he thought about how he and Michael had met. It was when Declan had been ejected from the force. He'd been escorted out of the police station by his senior partner Gary Sawchuck, who had stayed by Declan's side as he had cleared out his locker in anticipation of his firing or worse, a potential jail sentence. They'd ended up at Sawchuck's favourite pub far away from the station and it was there that Sawchuck had admitted he had no respect for the cop that Declan had beaten up. After all, the guy was clearly a bigot and had been waiting for a reason to pick a fight with Declan. The guy just hadn't anticipated that Declan's response would leave him so badly injured.

Sawchuck had said that whatever had triggered the rage in Declan — a rage that had resulted in Declan nearly beating the man to death — it had to be dealt with. He had suggested that Declan should seek out the help of a therapist as soon as possible. It would help him with his anger and would also look good to the board of inquiry which would undoubtedly be contacted regarding the incident. Sawchuck had placed a call then and there and arranged for Declan to see Michael.

"I think you'll find you two have a lot in common," he'd said.

Declan wasn't sure if Sawchuck was setting up a therapy session or a date. He should have known better.

Michael, it turned out, was a woman. She specialized in trauma and had treated a lot of cops. Michael's wife had been an officer who was on the drug squad working undercover. She had been killed in a raid and through the process of dealing with her own grief, Michael had told Declan that she'd discovered that she had a gift for comforting her wife's colleagues. She had revealed that it was at that moment that she'd decided to help other cops deal with their trauma.

Declan recalled that during his first session, Michael had told a story about her given name. Her mother had always loved that name for a woman. When Michael had come out of the closet, her mother had been concerned that the name she'd chosen for her daughter had done something to cause her to become a lesbian. It took her a good year to convince her mother that she *went lesbian* all by herself. The thing about Michael was that she understood how a difficult relationship with a parent could twist someone around for a long time when it came to being gay.

Declan remembered a lot about the early sessions with Michael. He had found her one of the easiest people in the world to talk to. By their third or fourth meeting, he had completely broken down in front of her, something he'd never done before. He was nothing but a puddle of tears talking about his father and the way he could turn Declan into a quivering child just by walking through the door. Michael had given him the tools to control his feelings and with each session, Declan had taken a step closer to leaving his childhood fears behind.

Declan shook himself free of his thoughts, and when he looked up, discovered he was already outside of Michael's building. He opened the door and made his way into the waiting room. Right on time.

Michael poked her head out of her office. "Come on in."

He followed her in and gave her the flowers. "Happy birthday," he said.

"You never forget. Thank you. Now tell me, how come you know my favourite flowers?"

Declan smiled. "You're not the only one who listens during our sessions. I remember you talking about the flowers you had on your wedding day."

Declan sat down on a chair, and waited as Michael poured two glasses of water from a pitcher, put the flowers in the remaining water in the pitcher then set the glasses in front of them. She sat down and referred to her notes.

"So," she started, "have you given any thought to what we talked about last time?"

He shook his head and smiled. "I am fucked," he said. "Charlie knows about you."

"Good," Michael said. "Did you tell him what we discussed on Monday?"

"Not exactly," Declan replied. "He doesn't know *who* you are, he just knows I'm seeing someone named

Michael. He saw your text after our appointment. He made some assumptions."

"So why didn't you clear those assumptions up?"

Declan rubbed his temples with the tips of his fingers like he was having a bad headache. "I didn't want him to know I was in therapy. It just opens up a whole conversation I'm not sure I want to have."

Michael took a sip of her water. "A conversation about why you're seeing a therapist, or a conversation about how, on our last visit, you expressed that you were falling in love with him?"

Declan massaged his temples a little faster.

"We're here so you can be honest with yourself and others," Michael said. "So tell me what you're so afraid of? What's the worst that could happen?"

Declan threw up his hands and confessed, "If something happened between us, I could lose him."

"Who, the person you love, or the person who's your employee?"

Declan was nervous when the word 'love' came up in regards to Charlie. He froze when the word came out of Michael's mouth, then sagged back into the chair and said, "Either."

"Okay. So, maybe you should start a relationship with Charlie and hire another office boy."

"I can't fire Charlie, and I don't want another office boy. Charlie is…perfect."

"Then, I repeat—what are you so afraid of?"

Declan closed his eyes. "That if I admit to him that I'm in love with him and he finds out how fucked up I am, he'll run."

She leaned forward in her chair. "From what you've told me he probably already knows how fucked up you are, and he still seems to want to be with you. Frankly, that has me far more worried about him than you."

Declan laughed.

"And how would you feel if you did nothing and he found someone else? He can't wait for you forever. How do you think it would feel working with him then?"

"I don't know."

"I think you do."

Declan shifted uncomfortably in his seat.

"What is it?" she asked.

"What if something happens to him? I mean, something really bad?"

"You mean what happens if he gets hurt or killed?"

"Yes," Declan whispered.

Michael looked towards the flowers. "Charlie could get hit crossing the street, or just wind up in the wrong place at the wrong time. There's nothing you can do to prevent that. He's got to make his own decisions."

She paused until Declan looked up at her. "You can spend your whole life worrying about the worst-case scenario, or you can let both of you make the decision. Too many people miss out on too much life because they're afraid to take a risk. My recommendation — tell him the truth."

Declan closed his eyes again and clenched his lips.

"But that's not what this is about, is it?" Michael asked.

Declan knew what she was getting at, but he wasn't ready to say it.

"I know you well enough to know that you don't run away from anything. That's how you've gotten each and every one of those scars on that body of yours. In fact, you seem to get some weird pleasure out of putting yourself in positions where you get the shit kicked out of you. It seems like you think that if you're in physical pain, you won't have to deal with your emotional pain. Declan, I think for once it's time that you put yourself in the way of being emotionally hurt."

"Emotional hurt is what brought me here in the first place."

"And you've been running from it since you were a child. Time for tough talk. You need to face up to your feelings towards Charlie like the other things you've faced over the years. And if you can't deal with it, then maybe you should consider severing ties before you hurt him. Whatever you decide, the sooner you do something, the better."

Declan stared down at the floor. In his heart, he knew what he had to do.

Chapter Twenty-Two

Charlie sat at Declan's desk. He liked the feeling of being at his own desk, in his own private office, interviewing his own clients. He began to type up his report on the Cody White interview. First impressions—he had been nervous, and not just because he was being interviewed. Cody had chewed his fingernails down to the quick and, from the dried blood on some of his cuticles, he had been doing so for some time. Also, Cody had seemed more concerned about his mother than himself...

Charlie continued transcribing his written notes, ensuring that the key points were captured in detail, then he began to listen to the recording he'd made. There might be something more in that. By the time he was finished, Charlie had compiled a hefty document of what had transpired. He would show Declan that he could handle situations like this on his own.

Charlie looked at the time on his phone. It was almost six o'clock and there had still been no response from Declan. He tapped out a quick message.

Just checking. Did you get my last text about Cody White and Tull and Monarch? Is everything okay?

Charlie hoped there would be an immediate ping back, but nothing. This was important. Why wasn't Declan answering him? No point in worrying. Maybe he was just running late from whatever his other business was, but Charlie wanted to be here when he got back.

To distract himself, Charlie thought back on what Cody had said about meeting Tull on an S&M online hookup site. Charlie wondered if he could find which one Tull had used, and what it might tell Charlie about him. He hadn't thought to ask Cody which site it was, so he'd have to do a bit of digging. In a matter of minutes Charlie had discovered five popular sites. He went onto the top-ranked one, *Chaps-n-Slaps*, and discovered that to access any of the user profiles, he had to create an account. Charlie settled on *ComputerHustler* as his username.

He was surprised to find that there were close to a thousand members in Alberta. There was a range of profiles, but to get detailed pictures or information, the user had to request permission from the person they were interested in. As Charlie surfed through the profiles, he discovered that one of the users was *SmoothStud123*. Next he looked for *BakuBondageBoy*, Tull's email username. There he was. This was the site! Charlie was on a roll.

"Well, let's see how lucky I am," he said to himself.

He filtered his search by men in the Drumheller area and searched for the other file that had been on Tull's computer — *BurlyBiker27*. Nothing. He shouldn't have been surprised. Cody, after all, was from Calgary, not Drumheller, and Tull's other visitors could have been from other places outside of Drumheller. Charlie expanded his search to all of Alberta. He skimmed through the profiles and eventually hit pay-dirt. There was the profile for *BurlyBiker27* but there was no image on his user icon. And in order to access more of his profile, *BurlyBiker27* required that you send him a full nude shot. Charlie wasn't about to have a dick-pic of himself floating around on the web, so there'd be no images of the third blackmail victim this evening.

Charlie stared at the screen.

"Wait a minute. You idiot," Charlie said to himself.

He already had a picture of the guy he knew as *BurlyBiker27*. Charlie had a whole video's worth of just about every square centimetre of him. And if he had a picture...Charlie was struck with a new idea.

He called up the video for *BurlyBiker27* on his laptop. It showed two men involved in sex play. One of them had a dark bushy beard and was lying in the sling. The other, who was penetrating him, wore a leather mask which hid his identity. The two men had their hands around each other's throat and were clearly choking one another. Charlie stopped the video and zoomed in on the masked man. There was a tattoo of a spider on his left forearm.

Charlie continued to scan through the video until he found the clearest possible shot of the face of the man who was in the sling. He took a screen-capture of it. Then, Charlie did an internet image search.

In a short period of time, images started to pop up, dozens of them. Then hundreds of images that the search engine's algorithms determined looked similar to the one Charlie had hoped to match.

The image Charlie had asked the computer to find matched a lot of different men, as the man's bushy beard hid a lot of facial features which would have been helpful in narrowing the search. Charlie played with the image, focusing more on the man's eyes, nose and mouth then narrowed his search to images posted within the last five years.

This brought it down to a manageable one hundred and fifty-three images. Charlie began to scroll. After a few minutes, Charlie found what he was looking for.

"Oh shit."

There was no doubt about it. This had to be *BurlyBiker27*. Charlie was staring at an image from an Edmonton Police Service post from 2020. It was a plea to the public looking for information on the whereabouts of "Adolph Moses. Age forty-two. Height one-hundred-and-ninety centimetres. Weight one-hundred-and-seven kilos. Warning—this man is armed and dangerous. Do not approach. Call…"

Charlie stared at the image of the man's face. His eyes looked crazed. His hair was a tangled mess. He had the same beard as the guy in the video—a full biker beard.

Biker beard.

Biker.

"No way," Charlie said as he grabbed his phone and called up the images in his photos folder. He scrolled through them quickly until he came to the one he'd taken of the biker they'd seen on the road near Hoodoo House. He zoomed in on the face. He couldn't be absolutely sure. The helmet and goggles obscured the details, but there, on the biker's left cheek, just below the eye, was a tattoo of some sort. Charlie looked back at the video and advanced through it until he could see the left side of the man's face. There, on his cheek, was a tattoo below the left eye. A double teardrop. The same as the one on the face in the police bulletin.

This must be *BurlyBiker27*, the same guy who had threatened to kill Tull in the emails.

Charlie grabbed his phone and called Declan. The phone rang three times, then went to voicemail.

"Declan. It's Charlie. I've found out who *BurlyBiker27* is. This is big. Call me. Please!"

He disconnected. Where could Declan be?

Charlie looked at the cold coffee on his desk and decided to rinse out the mug and use the washroom. As he washed his hands, he caught a glimpse of himself in the mirror. He was a rumpled mess. He'd slept in his clothes the night before and hadn't shaved. He couldn't believe he'd interviewed Cody looking like this. He needed to get home. Declan could call him if he was interested in what Charlie had found out.

Home! Charlie realized he hadn't even taken the time to let Carrie know he was back in town. He shot off a quick text.

Homeward bound! Have the wine ready. I've got stories.

Within a minute, she texted back.

At work until ten. See you when I get home. Can't wait to hear what you and your Hot Dick have been up to.

Hot Dick. Charlie shook his head.

See you at ten.

Charlie locked the Cody White file away in a drawer, turned off the lights then set the alarm. He'd just started down the street towards the car when his phone rang.

He glanced at the caller ID.

"Declan! I've got news!"

"Yeah," Declan replied. "I just saw that. Great work. Listen. Can you meet me at Bar-None? There's something I need to talk to you about and it can't wait."

"Sure," Charlie replied. "I'll be there soon."

As he disconnected, Charlie's stomach began to churn. Declan sounded upset, and Charlie had a feeling that whatever he wanted to talk to him about, it wasn't the case.

Chapter Twenty-Three

Henry knew that Gramma Carol would be home eventually, and she wouldn't go easy on him if he hadn't finished his homework. He couldn't put it off any longer. He stowed the leather mask and shiny baton under his bed.

Then his stomach grumbled. Well, he couldn't do his homework with all of that noise going on down there. He'd better have a snack first.

Henry skipped his way to the staircase and decided to save time by sliding down the banister. This time he was smart enough to stop himself before he hit the newel post. That was a mistake a guy only made once on the staircase ride.

As he dismounted, the kitchen phone rang. He ran to get it. A good receptionist always answered a business phone after the second ring. Never before — that could startle the caller who was used to tardy receptionists, and never after more than three — that could anger some callers and you would just have to hang up on them and all their yelling, which was bad for business. Henry was determined to be the best receptionist Hoodoo House had ever had.

"Good evening, Hoodoo House. Henry Quill speaking. How may I direct your call?"

"Gimme the old lady who runs the place," said a deep, gruff voice.

"I assume you are referring to Gramma Carol? I'm afraid that she is out for the evening, but she'll be back in a few hours," Henry said, trying to hide his annoyance at someone referring to her as the 'old lady'.

The caller on the other end disconnected.

"Rude," Henry said into the phone receiver before hanging up.

Henry started to head back up to his room to work on his homework when his stomach reminded him of why he had come downstairs in the first place. He went to the fridge and piled a plate high with some of his Gramma Carol's fresh baked rolls, cold cuts which he rolled up to look fancy and a couple of peeled hard-boiled eggs.

Henry was about to make his way back to his bedroom when he realized something was missing. He needed something to drink. It took ten minutes for the new coffee to brew. Once it was done, Henry picked up a very full cup of coffee in one hand and an overloaded plate in the other then headed slowly and carefully back upstairs to his room.

It took three times as long going upstairs as it had coming down. His coffee kept trying to slop out of his mug and, on two occasions, he had to stop to retrieve the hard-boiled eggs when they escaped his plate. He tried brushing them off to no avail, so he decided to rinse them off in the bathroom sink instead.

Once everything was safely placed on the floor beside his bed, and the eggs were washed free of most of the floor fluff and grit, Henry began his homework. He gathered up the copies of *The Ragtag Crew* book and manuscript and began to write his essay. After fifteen minutes, he decided to go back downstairs and get a refill on his coffee. A mind must be kept sharp if it was to be creative!

Coffee acquired, he got back to work and examined his progress. Three paragraphs done! He finished three more paragraphs before taking another break to get some cookies and a top-up on his coffee. No wonder adults drank it. It made everything so sharp and exhilarating. His heart was racing with excitement.

Henry started having difficulty focusing.

What would The Slithe do if he had a really boring essay to write?

Henry took the leather mask and baton back out from under the bed. He put on the mask and stared hard at the words he'd written in his notebook. Nothing. Maybe if he practised more of his martial arts moves, it might get the blood flowing to his brain and great thoughts would come to him.

After a few minutes of kicking and spinning, he collapsed on the bed, exhausted. He slipped the mask off his head and lay there in silence. Then he heard something. What was that buzzing sound? It seemed to be coming from outside and it was getting louder…like a giant fly.

Henry needed to go and take a look.

He padded down the hallway and opened the broom closet, then pushed open the secret door to the tower and climbed the steps to the lookout. The sun was setting and it was difficult to make out anything.

Difficult, but not impossible. In the distance, he saw a single light and it was coming Henry's way. It was a motorcycle and Henry recognized it. It was the loud bike, the one that the big, hairy guy rode — the guy who one time had threatened to hurt Henry if he'd ever caught him touching his bike.

The bike came up the drive, then out of view and around the side of the house.

Henry had to act, and fast.

He ran down the wobbly tower stairs so quickly he thought they might break free from the walls. He had to find out what the man was going to do. He had a bad feeling about this.

Henry made his way through the back of the broom closet and edged open the door. He thought the coast was clear. Then he heard breaking glass.

Henry knew he should hide, but his coffee-fuelled brain told him he had to see what was happening. After all, he was the only one here, which made him responsible for the house, his and Gramma Carol's home.

He ran to his room and headed towards his closet. Like the broom closet, it had a secret panel at the back. It led into the passages — the ones that ran through the thick walls of the house, walls that had spy holes in them. Henry had laughed when people said they felt like they were being watched when they were in the house. They were — by him.

He made his way through the narrow space between the walls and down the crude wooden ladder to the first floor. From his hiding space at the back of the house he looked through a knothole in the wood and into the kitchen. The outer kitchen door had been broken open and Henry could hear smashing sounds coming from somewhere else in the house.

He scampered between the main floor walls to the front of the house where he could see his puzzle table through a spy hole. No one there! He continued on towards the noise. It was coming from the direction of the writing room.

Still safely hidden, he peered through holes that looked out into the main hall across from the room where Mr Tull had died. The door to the room lay on the floor, splintered. Through the opening to the room, Henry saw a chair go flying by. Then, a body stepped into view. It was a massive man, all hair and muscle crammed into leather. It was the giant that rode the big motorcycle.

All of a sudden the intruder's true identity was clear to Henry. How could he have not seen it before?

He looked like…no, he was *Momrath!*
He must be defeated once and for all!

Henry went back through the passageways, up the ladder and exited the closet into his bedroom. He picked up the leather mask and zipped it onto his head. He saw himself in the mirror. The Slithe looked back at him.

While Henry would have been afraid, The Slithe was not. He could not be. He was a superhero, one who armed himself with a black leather baton and his trusty…Henry looked around for his *bo* staff, the weapon of choice for the warrior that he was. There, in the corner of the closet, was an old pool cue that Henry had found years ago and tucked away. That would do.

This was the moment The Slithe was born for.

He quietly made his way to the stairs. The crashing sounds had changed. They no longer came from the writing room.

Henry carefully crept down the staircase to the main floor, avoiding the creaking treads which were mapped out in his mind. When he reached the third step from the bottom, he was startled by the sound of the red velvet curtains at the entrance to the puzzle room being torn from their rod. Out stepped Momrath.

Henry stood face to face with his arch-nemesis. Henry would have been terrified. But The Slithe... The Slithe knew how to handle guys like this, whoever they were.

The monster stared at Henry. He looked surprised. The Slithe suspected he had the upper hand.

"What the fuck are you supposed to be?" the intruder demanded.

"I am your worst nightmare, Momrath. I am The Slithe."

"The what?" he said as he advanced on Henry.

The Slithe grabbed the baton from his belt and flung it at his enemy.

There was a cracking sound as the weapon shattered the bridge of Momrath's nose, followed by a scream of pain mixed with rage. Blood gushed with force from the man's nostrils.

Henry yelled in his cracking pubescent voice, "Momrath, you have been smited!" The intruder charged towards him. Henry, out of instinct, backed up and snagged the heel of his foot on a step. As he tumbled backward, the pool cue in his hand got wedged between the riser and the tread of the stair. The intruder dove towards Henry, hitting the old pool cue with so much force that it splintered and dug deep into his shoulder. Blood sprayed everywhere. Momrath's screams echoed throughout the house.

Henry ran up the stairs, then slipped into the broom closet and made his way into the secret tower room. He could still hear Momrath raging down below.

"I'm going to get you, you little fucker. And then you're going to tell me where Tull hid that computer."

From the safety of the tower, Henry saw a car coming up the drive. He recognized the fins of Lem Franklin's Coupe de Ville. It was clear that the intruder had also heard the car, for a few seconds later, the motorcycle started up and drove away.

As soon as he thought it was safe, Henry ran down the stairs.

Gramma Carol came through the front door. She flicked on the hall light and stared in horror at the smashed-up writing room and the blood sprayed up the wall. She looked down to the broken, blood-covered pool cue which lay on the floor.

"What the… Henry!" she called out.

All of the strength of The Slithe vanished. Henry launched himself at his gramma, and held on to her tightly.

"Gramma Carol, I think you need to call the police."

Chapter Twenty-Four

Declan sat at his usual table at the back of Bar-None. He felt safe here, not that he was expecting anyone to sneak up from behind and knife him. It was just that here he knew he could have a private conversation with the fewest people listening in. And if the conversation ended badly, Declan could always sneak out of the bar through Mickey's office, which was right beside him.

He saw a mop of unruly blond hair working its way through the crowd.

"Hey," Charlie said as he sat down across from him. His face was filled with concern. "So," Charlie started, "you get my texts?"

"I did!" Declan said with forced enthusiasm.

"And the big news is that *BurlyBiker27* is someone who's wanted by the police. His name is Adolph Moses. And in my interview with Cody White—he's being blackmailed. He's *SmoothStud123*. And his case is connected to a trial involving Monarch."

"That's good work, Charlie."

Charlie detected an odd tone in Declan's voice. "Did I do something wrong?" Charlie asked. "I thought you'd be really interested in all of this."

"I am. More and more it's starting to appear that Malcolm Tull's death wasn't accidental. He had enough enemies who had a motive, and there's evidence on the victim's computer—the emails and videos, and a nice selection of identifiable culprits."

"Why didn't you return my texts or call?" Charlie interjected.

Declan paused. He knew this conversation would be difficult—he just hadn't anticipated how difficult it would be until now. "I have something I need to talk to you about."

Charlie looked down at his drink. "I was wondering when we'd be having this discussion. This is about Michael, isn't it?"

"Yes."

"Have you been lovers for a long time?" Charlie asked.

The hurt in Charlie's voice was soul crushing.

"Charlie. It's not what you think."

"Isn't it?"

Declan reached over and put his hands on Charlie's. "Charlie, look at me."

Charlie remained motionless.

"Look at me, please."

Charlie looked up. His cheeks were damp with tears.

"Charlie. Michael's not my lover. They're my therapist. And, to top it off, Michael's a woman."

"What?"

"And a tougher dyke you wouldn't find at a rodeo," Declan said with a smile.

"She's a…"

Declan saw a slight glimmer returning to Charlie's eyes. "She's been helping me ever since I got kicked off of the police force. *Trying* to help me would be a better word for it—with my anger towards my father, the cops...myself. And now she's helping me deal with my feelings towards you."

"Your...feelings towards...me?" Charlie's tears continued.

"She's pushing me to jump in with both feet."

"Why didn't you tell me about her in the first place?" Charlie asked. "Don't you trust me?"

"Trust you? You're one of the few people I *do* trust. Look, I've had a lifelong habit of throwing roadblocks in front of myself whenever things are going well. I'm just a bit fucked up and I didn't want you to find out about it. At least not yet."

"So what does this mean?"

Declan replied, "I think I have to fire you."

Charlie's face fell as he slumped back into his chair and his shoulders sagged. "But why?"

"I care too much about you to let you get hurt. Maybe if you aren't working for me, we can approach the relationship without all the complications."

"But I'm good at my job. I love my job. I love...you. And in terms of keeping me out of danger, that's *my* decision to make. I'll brush up on my karate. I'll...learn how to punch things! Besides, most of my work is in the office, which is hardly life-threatening." Charlie leaned in close to Declan. "I want to make this work. I know we can do it."

"Charlie, I've been making a lot of bad decisions lately, and this decision is a big one."

"And *I've* been making a lot of good decisions lately, and I'm not going to let this stop me. Did Michael tell you to fire me so we could have a relationship?"

"Not exactly. She said I was afraid to take emotional risks."

Charlie looked at Declan intently. "What do you *really* want?"

Declan swirled the drink in front of him, then knocked it back. "What the hell." He stood up, walked around the table, leaned over and kissed Charlie on the mouth. It was a long, passionate kiss. Charlie kissed him back.

"Come on," Declan said, grabbing Charlie by the hand. "I've been waiting too long for this."

They ran like they were being chased by a pack of wolves, through the crowded bar and out onto the street. Declan heard Charlie laughing. He hailed a nearby cab and within minutes they were climbing the stairs to the office.

As they burst through the office door, Declan grabbed Charlie and kissed him again. The moment was broken by a loud shrill noise that filled the air. They both dove for the security panel, simultaneously trying to punch in the code before the security company was called.

"Here, just let me..." Charlie said, pushing Declan aside.

Ten seconds later there was silence.

They turned again to face each other. This time Charlie grabbed Declan by the shirt-front and pulled him in, kissing him gently, then more deeply. Their tongues caressed each other.

"Come on," Declan said, taking Charlie by the hand and leading him to the bed upstairs.

Declan took his time undressing Charlie. He undid his shirt, one button at a time, meticulously stripping his slender shoulders and smooth chest. As he peeled the shirt off of him, he leaned into his torso, and kissed his neck, then his shoulders, then stooped to kiss his chest. He dipped Charlie's body back, as a dancer would dip his partner, then bent forward until his lips brushed against Charlie's nipples, which had hardened with the first touch of his breath.

This was different than Declan's other sexual encounters which were forceful, overpowering and all about taking control over the other man's body. With Charlie, each touch was a gentle caress, whether it was with his lips or his fingers. Charlie was someone to be worshipped, not conquered.

Declan dropped to his knees. His tongue traced the path from Charlie's navel, down the light trail of hair that ran towards his waist. He expertly removed Charlie's belt and unbuttoned the waistband of his pants. He gripped the fly-tab with his teeth and lowered it, letting his nose graze the cotton of Charlie's briefs. The scent of the sweat on Charlie's pubic hair filled his nostrils and caused his pulse to race.

Declan rid him of his pants, then, still kneeling before him, slid his underwear over the mounds of his ass, freeing his hard cock which shot upwards and slapped the underside of Declan's chin, surprising him and Charlie. They both burst out laughing.

Declan stood, and started to tickle Charlie, throwing him into hysterical laughter, before he picked him up and tossed him onto the bed.

Declan peeled his own tight-fitting clothes off of his muscled body, slowly removing his pants and underwear. He crawled up from the foot of the bed and hovered above Charlie, stopping only to swallow his cock to the root for a moment, then continued upwards until they were face-to-face. The young man's smile was angelic. Declan gently kissed him, then lowered himself onto Charlie's erection. Declan's eyes widened and his mouth dropped open in ecstasy. He knew then that nothing was ever going to be the same again.

* * * *

In the morning, Charlie lay with his head on Declan's chest. He could hear Declan's heart pounding. The two were damp with sweat, as were the sheets.

He ran his fingers through Declan's chest hair. It was as black as night. Declan leaned in, kissed him on the head and held him close.

Charlie fell silent. He was worried. He pressed his head further into the cradle between Declan's arm and chest.

"What's wrong?" Declan asked.

Charlie sat up looking towards the end of the bed, then, finding his courage, looked Declan in the face.

"Was I okay?" Charlie asked.

"Okay?"

"You know. In bed? I didn't bore you, did I?"

"Why would you say that?"

"Because...you know. You've had a lot of guys to compare me with."

"I wouldn't say that," Declan replied.

"Survey companies would be thrilled to have your sample size—oh my God!" Charlie realized he had basically called Declan a whore. "I'm so sorry. I didn't mean it. I'm a terrible person and—"

Declan put his finger on Charlie's lips. "Shhh. You're working yourself up over nothing. You were perfect. And do you know why? Because you're Charlie

Watts. No one else can claim that. And if you're worried about technique…no one, and I mean no one has fucked me like that."

"Really?"

"This is gonna sound weird," Declan said, "but you did it with your whole body and soul. Most guys do it like they're jerking off. They do it just to come. You… you did it like you wanted to be a part of me, and that was special."

Charlie looked up at Declan. "Since you brought up the subject of skill, how did you get the condom on my cock? I certainly didn't do it."

Declan smiled. "We all have our secrets."

Charlie looked at him and raised a single eyebrow.

Declan finally confessed, "I popped it in my mouth after I got undressed. When I went down on you, I unrolled it as I went. Something I learned to do to protect myself a long time ago."

"That must have taken a lot of practise." Charlie rolled on top of Declan and stared at him intently.

Declan just smiled mysteriously.

Charlie pointed to the scar that cut through Declan's left eyebrow. "How did you get that?"

"That was when I was thrown into an open car door in my first week of police training."

"And that?" Charlie asked, stroking a three-centimetre-long scar between two ribs on Declan's right side.

"A knife. A junkie did that to me in a back alley when I was trying to get to his friend who was OD'ing."

Charlie sucked in air at the thought of it. "Ouch. How about that one?" he said, tracing his index finger around a broad, shiny ten-centimetre scar on Declan's inner right calf.

"That was my own fault. I got that when I learned

how hot a motorcycle exhaust pipe can get. Let that be a lesson to you – always wear long pants when you get on a bike. So, how about you?"

Declan pushed Charlie flat on his back. "You've gotta have war wounds somewhere. There," he said, pointing to Charlie's lower abdomen.

"Appendix. Hardly what I'd call a war wound."

Declan leaned down and kissed it, then began to tickle Charlie until he was hysterical with laughter again.

Declan's phone rang.

"Ignore it," Declan said. "I'm only interested in you right now."

Charlie looked over and noticed the caller ID. It was four letters. "I think you should take this."

Declan looked at the caller ID and scowled. "I need you to take this. Answer like you would if you were in the office."

Charlie nodded, then answered. "Declan Hunt Investigations. Charlie Watts speaking. How may I help you?"

Declan slid down the bed and started nibbling on Charlie's toes.

"Is Declan Hunt there, please?" a voice asked.

"I'm afraid he can't come to the phone at the moment," Charlie said, trying to control his breathing as Declan went to town.

"This is Sergeant Kaci Bowen from the RCMP, Drumheller detachment. We understand that Mr Hunt has been involved with an investigation at Hoodoo House, near Rosebud."

"Yes, we, I mean, Mr Hunt was working there." Charlie's voice went up an octave as Declan did something magical with his tongue.

"It's come to our attention that a computer was located on the premises and it's currently in Mr Hunt's possession. Tell Mr Hunt I'd like to see him and the computer in Drumheller no later than four p.m. today or we'll send someone to Calgary to retrieve it."

Chapter Twenty-Five

Charlie disconnected from the call.

Declan started working his way up from Charlie's toes.

Charlie sat up and pushed Declan's head away. "That was the RCMP, and they want us and Tull's computer in Drumheller by four this afternoon."

Declan frowned. "What the hell?"

"How did they find out about the computer?" Charlie asked.

Declan shrugged. "Not many options there. We must have a rat at Hoodoo House. Could have been any of them—Sinclair, Mrs Cameron or Henry. Probably not Sinclair, though. He doesn't want that video to come out."

Declan sat up. "And who knows? Maybe the cops heard about the computer through another investigation...but somehow I doubt it."

"Maybe I should give Hoodoo House a call and find out if anyone there said anything," Charlie replied as he turned on his side.

"Not a bad idea. Then we can grab a shower and maybe swing by your place and get you changed. You're looking a little…rumpled."

Charlie thumped Declan with a pillow, then grabbed his phone and called Hoodoo House. The call was picked up after two rings.

"Good morning, Hoodoo House, Hen—"

"Good morning, Henry," Charlie interrupted.

"Charlie! You wouldn't believe what happened last night. There was this big guy, I mean he was huge and he rides this massive motorcycle and he came smashing into the house yesterday—*crash!* And he started to bust up—"

"Henry. Slow down. I want you to take a deep breath and tell me, slowly, what happened."

"What's going on?" Declan whispered.

Charlie held up his hand.

"There was this big biker guy," Henry continued, now talking painfully slow. "He came to the house last night when Gramma Carol was away. He started to smash up the place…but I chased him away, smiting him like The Slithe smited Momrath in my comic books. It was so cool I wish you could have seen it!"

"Are you and Mrs Cameron all right?"

"Yup. Yup, right as rain. We're good," Henry piped.

"Is your Gramma Carol around?"

"She's having her bath right now. I could go and get her if you want."

"No, Henry, that's okay. Tell me—did the police come by last night?"

"You bet. They were here in a flash. And it was the same sergeant that came when Mr Tull died."

"Sergeant Bowen?"

"Yeah. That's her. She's really nice, though she wouldn't let me sit in the front of the police car. Speaking of cars, you still owe me a ride in yours. It's way cooler than Sergeant Bowen's."

Declan looked at Charlie intently.

"I'll fill you in in a second," Charlie whispered to Declan, then turned his attention back to the call.

"Did Sergeant Bowen ask about us, by any chance?" Charlie pressed.

There were a few seconds of silence on the phone before Henry spoke. "Yeah...I think I may have told them that you were here looking for a missing computer."

"And did you tell her we found it?" Charlie continued.

"I might have," he said. "She asked if I had any idea what the man who broke in was looking for, and I may have mentioned the computer. Please don't be mad at me, Charlie. I didn't mean to tell."

"No, it's okay, Henry. No one's mad at you. We're just glad that everyone is okay. Look, we have to meet with the RCMP in Drumheller this afternoon. After we're done, is it okay if we come to Hoodoo House and check up on everyone?"

Charlie whispered to Declan, "That's okay, isn't it?"

Declan nodded.

"I'd like that," Henry replied. "The police still have some stuff they want to do, but you could come out later in the day."

"See you about six then? And make sure you tell Gramma Carol we're coming."

"You bet!" Henry said. "Charlie, will I get that ride in your car?"

"Maybe. We'll see you at six."

Charlie disconnected the call and took a deep breath.

"I take it something went down last night at Hoodoo House involving the police?" Declan asked.

Charlie nodded. "Someone attacked the house. Henry said he fended off the intruder, although he was so excited by it all, I'm not sure what really happened. The police came and everyone seems to be all right."

"Well, at least we know how the cops found out about the computer."

"Henry said that the guy who attacked them was big and rode a large motorcycle."

Declan pursed his lips. "*BurlyBiker27?*"

"Maybe. Declan, if he was capable of tearing the place apart, maybe he *was* involved in Malcolm Tull's death. After all, the email on the computer shows he threatened to kill him."

Declan scowled. "Something still isn't sitting right with me about Malcolm Tull's death, but I'm sure it has to do with that computer and what's on it. Maybe Tull really did take his own life for some reason — out of fear. You know, he killed himself before someone else did it for him? Although I'm not really convinced about that. We haven't seen any evidence that would push an egomaniac like him to commit suicide. What seems more likely is that someone killed him to shut him up, and then tried to find the computer. But the biker seems a more violent type. He'd have been more likely to choke Tull to death or use a knife on him rather than to take his chances on poisoning him with an overdose of his medication."

"True," Charlie said.

Declan continued, "The evidence we've seen from the videos and emails points to either Sinclair or Cody White."

"They were both in the house around the time of Tull's death," Charlie added. "I mean, they had motive and they were both being threatened. But I still don't think Cody has it in him to be a killer. He could barely get through the interview without chewing his nails to the quick. Do you think he'd have the guts to do it?"

"I don't know. His behaviour around you could have been a result of guilt, or fear of being found out. It'd be nice to put him under pressure and see if he snapped. But even then…"

"And Sinclair raised a valid point that if he did kill Tull," Charlie continued, "it wouldn't make sense for him to hire you and risk being caught."

Declan sat up on the edge of the bed. "I'm not convinced that either of those guys did it. At least not enough that I'd be willing to put their necks in a noose. We don't have enough information yet. Maybe the RCMP can shed more light on what actually happened."

"So what do we do?" Charlie asked.

Declan paused for a moment. "We'll take in the computer and turn it over to the cops. First, though, I want you to scrub the manuscript and the video files with Cody White and Sinclair Yamada off the computer. Can you do that so there's no trace?"

"I guess," Charlie said. He didn't like the idea of tampering with evidence.

"We'll still have them on your backup server if we or the cops need them in the future," Declan assured him. "The only video we'll leave for now is the one for *BurlyBiker27*, who you identified as Adolph Moses. We'll see if the cops are willing to share any information they have about him. From what Henry told you, it's possible that it was him who attacked the house. I suspect the police would be interested in the connection anyway, and there's no reason to point them towards the others until we have proof that they were involved."

Declan smiled. "This is fun. Solving cases in bed together."

Charlie looked down at his hands. "Shouldn't we give everything we have to the RCMP?"

Declan gently took Charlie by the shoulders and looked him in the eyes. "We don't want innocent people to get hurt through this, and we also have to respect the confidentiality of our clients. Cody White is a client. Sinclair Yamada is a client. But *BurlyBiker27* is not. And I promise if we uncover something else that leads another direction, we'll find a way to turn over the backup files to the RCMP at the right time in the right way."

"Okay," Charlie said. "I should also clear the computer's search history of references to Tull's Proton account. That way we don't have to worry about the police stumbling across the emails from Sinclair and Cody. I'll still be able to access them later if we need them."

"Smart man," Declan said. "You get on that and I'll call Sinclair and ask him to meet us at Hoodoo House at six to fill him in on what we've found. Charlie, we'll get to the bottom of this one way or the other."

* * * *

The morning went by quickly as Charlie removed the files and backed them up to an encrypted site. Then he made his way home to Carrie, who gave him an earful for not texting, although she seemed less angry when she found out where Charlie had been. It was close to two o'clock by the time Charlie got back to the office.

"You all right if I drive today?" Declan asked. "I'm kinda enjoying the Beast."

"Sure." Charlie said.

"All right. Grab the computer and let's go."

Charlie paused. "Just one more thing. Meet me in the back parking lot by the car."

Ten minutes later, Charlie came out of the back door to Gwen's Café with coffees and a brown paper bag. He passed Declan his coffee through the driver's window.

"What's in the bag?" Declan asked.

"You and I are now part of an experiment," Charlie said. "Gwen's branching out into sandwiches and she wanted us to try some. I figured since we haven't had lunch…"

In a matter of minutes, the sandwiches were gone.

Declan passed Charlie his coffee, "No cupholders. I guess you still get to hold this. We'd better get on the road."

They made their way north along Highway 2 and, just past Airdrie, turned east onto secondary Highway 567. Charlie remembered his last time in Airdrie a few months ago, where the case they had been working on had taken a turn for the worse. He put the memory behind him and watched the prairie scenery go by.

As they turned north on Highway 9, Charlie noted a sign that said they were within forty-five minutes of Drumheller. The road continued in wide ninety-degree arcs which skirted fields of freshly harvested wheat. They kept heading east, then north then east, then south, until eventually the highway took a much sharper bend to the north. Charlie gasped as the ground dropped away from the farmers' fields. Where the flat lands should have continued, instead, a giant hole in the earth opened up and there was a maroon-striped gorge that appeared out of nowhere. It was Horseshoe Canyon. Charlie had been there a few times as a kid, but he'd forgotten how awe-inspiring it was. His reverie was interrupted by a loud roar.

A motorcycle raced by and pulled in front of the car. A second bike pulled up beside them, driving in the empty oncoming traffic lane, matching their speed.

"Declan?" Charlie said, trying not to sound overly concerned.

"I see 'em. And there's another one coming up our rear."

Charlie turned around and looked out through the back window. There he was — a biker in a black leather jacket, helmet and goggles. The first thing that came to mind was *Adolph Moses,* but the guy behind the car looked different. He had a long blond beard blowing back from his face.

"Charlie. Don't panic," Declan said calmly.

Charlie saw the biker on the driver's side of the car. He was aiming a handgun at Declan.

As Charlie tried to make himself as small as possible, an oncoming car came around the curve and blared their horn as they were forced onto the shoulder of the road. The biker didn't give an inch.

Charlie poked his head up and saw a sign for a parking lot coming up ahead. Declan said, "I'm pulling over. Do whatever they ask but do it slowly. No quick moves, okay?"

"Sure," was all that Charlie could muster.

The small motorcade pulled up to the viewpoint parking lot. Signs indicated that the lot was closed for the season. The biker in the lead managed to force the gate open then drove in. The biker that had been riding beside them, with a silver lightning bolt decal on his helmet, pulled in front and led the car in. In the rearview mirror, Charlie saw the blond bearded biker close the gate and follow. Once they'd come to rest at the edge of the canyon, the three bikers dismounted and approached the car, guns drawn.

"Charlie, do what I do," Declan said.

Declan unsnapped his seat belt and slowly opened his door. He raised his hands so the bikers could see that he had nothing in them. Charlie did the same. Both got out of the Beast.

The biker that had been in the lead motioned to Charlie to get around to the driver's side of the car.

The biker with the long blond beard tucked his gun into his belt and came up to Declan. He patted him down. Charlie assumed he was looking for a gun. He then did the same with Charlie.

"We'll make this simple," said Lightning Bolt, who seemed to be in charge. "You give us the computer, and you don't die."

Charlie felt like throwing up.

"Charlie," Declan said in a calm voice. "Give the man the laptop. Slowly."

"Right," was the only word he could come up with.

Declan looked at the biker and said, "It's in the back seat. My friend will have to crawl in to get it."

Lightning Bolt looked at the blond biker who had patted Declan down and said, "Watch him from the other side. If he does anything stupid, shoot him."

Charlie started to shake. Tears clouded his vision.

"I'll get it for him," Declan said. "I wouldn't want your friend to shoot, miss and accidentally take one of you out."

Declan motioned to Charlie to stand out of the way, then slowly reached into the car and flipped the seat latch, allowing the driver's seat to snap forward. Charlie winced at the violent motion of the car seat. Declan remained calm. He reached into the back seat and lifted out the laptop. He backed up. "Can I ask what this is all about?"

Charlie screamed in his head, *Don't talk to them. Just make them go away!*

Lightning Bolt said, "All you need to know is that Monarch's been watching. They know all about that old house you've been visiting. And they know you've got the computer. They've got eyes everywhere and nothing escapes them."

Declan nodded and handed Lightning Bolt the computer.

Charlie hadn't moved a muscle. He focused on Declan. Declan nodded at him. Charlie wasn't sure if he was trying to tell him everything would be okay or if it was more of a *it's been nice knowing you. Sorry about this.*

Charlie watched Lightning Bolt walk to his bike and put the laptop into the pannier on the back. The biker who'd opened the gate to the parking lot mounted his own bike. The last to saddle up was the blond. Charlie was starting to feel that they might not die, when the blond pulled his gun out of the waistband of his pants.

Charlie closed his eyes and waited for the pain. He heard a gunshot, then the roar of the motorcycles starting up and departing. He carefully opened his eyes, expecting Declan to be lying on the ground, but Declan wasn't there. Then from behind him Charlie felt a hand on his shoulder. He jumped.

"It's all right. You're okay. You did well," Declan said.

Charlie felt Declan's arms around him.

"They're gone now. I'm so proud of you. You did everything you were supposed to do."

"I don't feel like I did."

"You did better than I did the first time this sort of thing happened to me," Declan replied. "And you did better than the Beast."

"What do you mean?" Charlie asked.

Declan turned Charlie around and showed him the car. The back right tire was flat.

"He shot my car! That fucking asshole shot my car!"

"Yup."

"What do we do now?" Charlie asked.

Declan shrugged. "I figure there's no point in calling the police. We might as well just change the tire and keep our appointment. This puts things in an entirely different light."

Chapter Twenty-Six

Between the roadside attack and the time it had taken to change the tire, forty-five minutes had been added to the journey. It was close to four-thirty in the afternoon when Declan and Charlie pulled into the parking lot of the RCMP detachment in Drumheller. Before they left the car Charlie asked, "So what are we going to tell the police?"

"The truth."

"All of it?"

"All of the truth is such a...philosophical concept. Let's give the bare essentials. We found the computer, we were attacked today and we don't have the computer anymore. We'll bring in the shot-up tire as evidence. They may be able to run ballistics on the bullet I suspect is inside near the rim."

"And how do you know there'll still be a bullet inside?" Charlie asked.

"One entry hole. No exit," Declan said as he hauled the wheel out of the trunk. "I noticed it when I was changing the tire. You know, for a car that you claim to be your own, it seems strange that I was the one doing the dirty work."

Charlie smiled then reached over and squeezed Declan's biceps. "That's because you're the one with the necessary tools."

Declan grinned and shook his head.

They entered the front door of the RCMP Drumheller detachment building and walked up to the officer on duty. He looked up from the notes he was scribbling and said, "How can I help you?"

"We have a four o'clock appointment with Sergeant Kaci Bowen," Declan announced.

"You're a bit late, aren't you?" the officer said, sounding annoyed.

Declan hoisted up the wheel from the Beast and rested it on the edge of his desk. "Ran into a bit of gunfire on the way in."

Declan dropped it back onto the floor.

The officer made no comment as he picked up the phone.

"Yeah. Your four o'clock is here." He looked up at Declan and asked, "Names?"

"Declan Hunt and Charlie Watts."

The officer went back to the phone. "Yup. It's them. And from the looks of it, they brought you a gift."

He hung up. "You and your spare can wait over there," he said, pointing with his pen to a couple of seats off to the side.

Once they were seated, Charlie leaned over and whispered, "Do we tell them about the contents of the computer or about anything else we've found out?"

"Like I said before, just the essentials. Let me do the talking. I'll play it by ear and use the 'client confidentiality' line if I have to."

"Does that really work?"

"Not really. A wise-assed old man once told me 'Cop trumps private-eye every time.'"

"Your dad?" Charlie asked.

"Oh, yeah," Declan said, just as the inner door opened and a woman wearing a navy jacket and grey slacks entered the lobby.

"Mr Hunt?" she said, extending her hand.

"Sergeant Bowen," Declan said, standing and shaking the officer's hand. "This is my assistant, Charlie Watts.

"Mr Watts," she said and nodded. "And this is...what is this?" she asked pointing at the wheel.

"There's a story," Declan replied.

"I bet there is. Follow me."

Declan, carrying the wheel, and Charlie with his hands in his pockets, followed her to an office at the back of the main floor. She took a seat in an aged, duct-taped office chair behind her desk, and Declan and Charlie took the two chairs facing her.

"Coffee, gentlemen?"

"Love some. Thanks," Declan said.

Charlie followed with his own "Yes, please."

She stepped out of the office, and walked across the hall to a high-tech coffee maker. As she pressed a few buttons and the machine started to spew brown liquid into cups, Declan glanced at the paperwork spread over her desk. He saw a file labelled 'Tull, Malcolm. Hoodoo House'.

"Maybe I should help her," Charlie said, then left the office.

Declan turned to see Bowen trying to juggle three cups of hot coffee. He heard Charlie say, "Please. Let me help you with those."

Atta boy.

As they came back into the office, Bowen said to Charlie, "I couldn't live without this stuff. I'm sure my stomach must look like a sieve by now."

Charlie laughed, then passed a cup to Declan.

"Thanks," he said.

She edged her way around the desk and started, "So, before I ask you for the computer, I just want you to know why you've been called in here today. It appears we've both been looking into an incident that happened just under two weeks ago at Hoodoo House involving the suspicious death of a man named Malcolm Tull. I can't give you details of the investigation, but one of the loose threads that we've been trying to track down is Tull's missing computer. Last night, the house was broken into by someone who attacked the young boy who lives there. From what I understand, you've met the boy Henry?"

"We have," Declan said.

"The assailant said he was looking for a computer. We're working on the theory that this is the same computer that had been in the possession of Malcolm Tull. When we interviewed Henry last night, he said that there was a private detective who was also looking for the computer — that would be you — and apparently, you found it. Now, for obvious reasons, we're interested in finding out what in the world was on it that would interest a person badly enough to cause him to break into a house and threaten the life of a child. So what can you tell me?"

"What you've said is about right," Declan confirmed. "We were hired by Malcolm Tull's editor Sinclair Yamada to locate the computer, which supposedly held Tull's final manuscript on it. We found the computer yesterday."

"Good. You've saved us a lot of time then. I need to see the computer so that we can look at the contents."

"We're more than willing to comply with your request except for one slight problem," Declan said.

"Is this where you explain to me why you've brought me a car wheel instead of the laptop I requested?"

"Basically, yes," Declan said.

Sergeant Bowen nodded. "Go ahead, I can't wait to hear this one."

Declan explained what had happened on their way to Drumheller, giving details of the highway ambush, being forced off the road at gunpoint, the direct threat to his and Charlie's lives, and finally the shooting of the tire, everything as it actually happened.

Sergeant Bowen smiled. "That's the most imaginative variation on 'the dog ate my homework' that I've heard in my entire career."

Declan leaned forward and patted the tire. "Sergeant, I present to you evidence of our story. Inside this wheel I think you'll find the bullet that was fired by the biker in order to prevent us from following them. That's all I've got. Ballistics will find it, I'm sure. They may be able to even match it to a gun on record."

"Or match it to your own gun, Mr Hunt? I know that you're licensed to carry a firearm. You were issued it after you left the police force because of active threats to your life. It's in our files."

Charlie threw Declan a wide-eyed glance. "I didn't know that."

"Surprise!" Declan said.

"Did you use your weapon against your attackers

today?" she asked.

"I use it only on rare occasions when I think someone's life may be in danger. Otherwise, it sits in the safe at work, which is why I didn't have it with me today."

Sergeant Bowen stared at Declan. "If this crazy story is true—and it's wild enough that it might be—is there any chance that one of the men on the bikes was a tall, burly guy with a dark bushy beard? Because that's the way the boy described his attacker last night."

"No," Declan said. "The only one with a bushy beard was a blond. He seemed to be the one in charge. He had a helmet with a silver lightning bolt on it. But they may have been associated with the man you're describing."

Sergeant Bowen opened the Hoodoo House file and made some notes. Declan and Charlie sat quietly, sipping their coffees, glancing at each other.

"Okay, now, when the computer was in your possession, were you able to find what you were looking for?" she asked.

Declan decided it was easier at this point to lie. He shook his head. "The computer was password protected. Charlie was in the process of trying to get through the system's security in order to locate the missing manuscript, but he wasn't able to."

Bowen looked at Charlie and asked, "Is that something you're good at? Cracking passwords?"

"Obviously not good enough," Charlie answered, shrugging his shoulders.

"We have nothing to share with you right now," Declan continued, "but if we find anything that might be of use, we'll turn it over to the RCMP."

"Good," she said.

"Out of curiosity, with regard to the death of the Tull guy, do you suspect foul play?" Declan asked. "I'm just trying to assess the level of danger that my assistant and I might be facing."

"I can't say much at present. Now, getting back to your adventure, can you provide me with a complete description of the guys who threatened you?"

"Sure," Declan said and proceeded to describe them in as much detail as he could, which mostly connected to height and facial hair, since they had all been similarly dressed in biker leathers, goggles and helmets.

Sergeant Bowen typed up the description as Declan talked. When it was done, she printed it off, and Declan looked at the one-page report and signed off on it.

"I'm not sure if you want the tire," Declan said, "but the bullet in it might be of use. If you do examine it, I'd like it back when you're done. Those are expensive."

"I suppose it wouldn't hurt. Sit tight. I'll get you a receipt for the tire. In the meantime, I'll get them to put out a call to any cars on the road to be on the lookout for these bikers," she said, holding up Declan's description.

She took Declan's signed statement in one hand, picked up the wheel in the other like it weighed nothing and left the office.

The moment she was out of sight, Charlie reached over her desk and spun the Hoodoo House file around. He opened it, and used his phone to photograph the top two pages of the file. He closed the folder and rotated it back, taking his seat just before Sergeant Bowen returned.

"So, stay in touch and let me know if you hear any more about the computer," she said, handing them each a copy of her card. She gave Declan the receipt for his wheel. "I'll give you a shout when you can pick it up."

As she escorted them back to the front entrance, she asked, "So, are you fellows heading back to Calgary?"

"We have a meeting with the editor at Hoodoo House later today," Declan replied. "I don't think he'll be happy to learn that we lost the computer. We were planning on turning it over to him, but it's a matter for the publishers and the police to deal with now."

Declan and Charlie walked back to the Beast.

Declan said, "Thanks for playing along when they asked about the files on the computer. Speaking of files, grabbing those photos was a fast move on your part."

"I hope you didn't mind," Charlie said.

"Mind? I was impressed."

As Declan pulled the Beast out of the parking lot, Charlie called up the images he had quickly captured on the phone and started to read.

"This is interesting. It appears that the coroner has a good idea of what killed Malcolm Tull."

Declan said, "What did you find out?"

Charlie said, "Not so fast. I want to look at it more thoroughly. Why don't I share it with you once we get to Hoodoo House? I think everyone will find it very, very interesting."

Chapter Twenty-Seven

They refuelled the Beast at a nearby gas bar. The car was running on fumes when they pulled into the station. It was moments like this that Charlie was happy that this was a company car. The fill-up came in at a hundred and five dollars.

It was just before six p.m. when they made their way up the drive to Hoodoo House. All looked peaceful. Charlie and Declan got out of the car and took a quick look around the perimeter of the house. Where the entrance to the kitchen door had been, there was now a board and police tape. They walked around to the front door and knocked. There was no response. Declan knocked again, louder. The curtain covering the upper pane of glass parted and an eye peered out.

"Henry, would you let us in?" Charlie asked.

"Gramma Carol told me not to open the door under any circumstances."

"Henry, you know you can trust us."

The eye disappeared from the windowpane and

Henry opened the door, then quickly locked it once they were inside.

"Gramma Carol's just preparing some food," he said, then ran towards the back of the house.

As they walked down the hallway towards the kitchen, Charlie saw the door of the writing room lying in pieces on the floor. In its place, police tape crisscrossed the opening. The office furniture had been tossed around like a tornado had been through the room, and the books were stripped from the shelves. What Charlie found more disturbing was the wall that ran up beside the stairs. The wood panelling was stained with a spray of dried blood, along with bloody handprints. Charlie felt sick at the thought of thirteen-year-old Henry being involved in all of this.

When they reached the kitchen, Mrs Cameron stood by the stove stirring a large pot of soup. Charlie could smell freshly baked buns.

Henry stood close to Mrs Cameron.

He's probably still scared. Who could blame him?

"Come on. Sit down," she said. "I'm assuming you'll both eat."

"Thank you, Mrs Cameron. We'd love to," Declan replied.

There was a knock at the front door. Henry looked towards it, but didn't move.

"I'm closer," Charlie said. "I'll get it."

He opened the door and let Sinclair Yamada in.

"What a damned mess this has become," Sinclair said, looking around.

Charlie nodded and led Sinclair back to the kitchen.

They all sat down around the table like a dysfunctional family at Christmas. Mrs Cameron and Henry served. Sinclair tore his bun apart and started to shove it into his mouth. Henry cleared his throat. The young man lowered his head and said, "God, please bless this meal, and everyone around this table and the people they care about, both here and in heaven." He looked upward. "And Mom, I promise to eat all my soup, including the beans. Amen."

"Amen," Mrs Cameron said, followed by muttering from the others.

Declan began, "So we've got some news to share with you."

Mrs Cameron stared him down. "If you don't mind, before you share your news, can we just enjoy the food without talk of the recent nasty business? There'll be time enough to talk after we're done."

Declan nodded, and the only sound for the next ten minutes was the clattering of spoons on bowls, and Henry slurping his broth.

When the main meal was cleared away, Mrs Cameron brought out coffee and a sponge cake with whipped cream and strawberries.

Declan said, "Thank you Mrs Cameron. Is it all right to start now?"

She nodded.

"I have some bad news, Sinclair," Declan began. "The computer's been stolen."

"What!" Sinclair snapped.

Charlie interjected, "We had to turn it over to the RCMP anyway—"

Sinclair turned red in the face. "You turned the computer over?"

"We were going to—minus certain sensitive files as requested," Declan continued, "but we never got it to the cops. We were held up by a group of armed bikers who took the computer off our hands."

Sinclair thumped the table with his fist. "This whole thing is a bloody disaster."

"As I said," Declan reiterated, "certain sensitive files had been removed."

Sinclair scowled. "None of it matters anymore. Now that Malcolm Tull is dead, Mount Temple Press is seriously considering not continuing with the book series. The company's owner is well past his best-before date — his words, not mine — and he wants a break. He's currently looking at a take-over bid for the back-catalogue, and that's it. He'll be closing down operations."

"So how will this affect you?" Charlie asked.

"I'll be out on the street, looking for a job," Sinclair said. He took a sip of water then continued. "And as goeth Mount Temple Press, so goeth the Heart's Shadow Foundation. In a meeting earlier today, I found out that, in light of the potential sale and the recent events here, the foundation will begin winding down its operations. That includes the liquidation of all of its tangible assets. Hoodoo House will be sold, and there will be no more ghostwriters."

Henry looked panicked. "Mr Yamada — *shhh*," he said, putting his finger to his mouth. "You can't tell the secret. Declan and Charlie aren't supposed to know about the ghostwriters."

"They already do. I had to tell them," Sinclair snapped. "There comes a time when all secrets come out."

"How long have you known?" Declan asked Henry.

Henry pushed back from the table and stood up. "I saw what Mr Tull was writing and told Gramma Carol. She said we had to keep it a secret. We were never supposed to talk about this to anyone but ourselves.

She explained that, to the rest of the world, everything was written by Marjorie Ellis. We have to protect her legacy! And now it's all ruined because everyone's going to know."

Henry started to cry.

"Henry, Declan and I had to be let in on the secret," Charlie said. "It was important for us to know everything so we could find the last *Heart's Shadow* manuscript. And we've promised not to tell anyone."

"But Mr Yamada should have told me you knew!"

Sinclair raised his hands in the air. "Like I said, none of it matters anymore. Look around you. Tull is dead. A psychopath attacked the house, which put you and Mrs Cameron in danger. And there will be no more new *Heart's Shadow* books. All good things must come to an end."

Mrs Cameron stood up from the table. "They can't do this. They promised to keep the series alive as long as the sales were decent. And it's about more than money, Mr Sinclair. What about the readers? What about those poor people who look to *The Heart's Shadow* books as their escape from their humdrum lives? Surely the buyers will want to continue the series?" Mrs Cameron shook with anger. "And if the foundation gets rid of Hoodoo House, where will the boy stay? Where will I be left? This is *your* fault. If it wasn't for you, Tull would still be alive. I overheard your argument with Malcolm on the night that he died. It was a barn-burner. I've wondered since that day if it was you who somehow managed to get rid of him. I didn't hear clearly, but I did hear the word *blackmail*."

Sinclair's face hardened into a mask of fury. "If we're pointing fingers here, Mrs Cameron, according to what the police told me, Malcolm Tull likely died of an overdose of primidone, which was found in his glass of *kumis*. Isn't that something that *you* always prepared for him? I know that you had no love for Malcolm Tull. Maybe you should have thought about the consequences of your actions before you spiked his drink."

Mrs Cameron marched up to Sinclair and leaned in close to his face. "He had no respect for Marjorie Ellis. He was destroying her creation, unlike Thomas Pritchard who carried forward the original tone of her work. It was one thing to have to abide the disdain he had for the thing that kept a roof over his head – it was another thing to have to tolerate the company of the shady men he…associated with."

"So you did kill him?" Sinclair demanded.

"No, but a small part of me wishes I'd had the courage to do it."

"Now why would you say that?" Declan asked.

Suddenly it all made sense to Charlie. He turned to Mrs Cameron and said, "Perhaps because you *are* Marjorie Ellis."

The room went very still.

Then Henry cried out, "I knew it! Gramma Carol – you are, aren't you?"

Mrs Cameron looked directly at Henry and said, "No. That's not true."

"It is true. I can prove it," Henry said, then ran from the room.

"Henry!" she cried out. Mrs Cameron shook her head. "I don't know what's gotten into that boy."

They heard the sound of Henry's footsteps running up the main stairs, then back down again. He appeared at the door to the kitchen. In his hand he held a picture of three women. Charlie remembered that he'd seen the photo on his tour of the house. It had been taped to Henry's dresser mirror. Henry brought the picture to the table.

"What's this all about?" Mrs Cameron asked.

"You gave this to me. And there's three people in the picture." He pointed at it. "That's Gramma Rachael, that's your sister Florry and then there's you. It is you, isn't it? The third person?"

"Of course, Henry, you know that's me."

"And here," Henry continued, "see how it's labelled?"

He indicated the words written on the back — 'RACHAEL, FLORRY, & ME'.

"It's like a puzzle, isn't it?" Henry said. "ME are the initials for Marjorie Ellis. I never said anything, because I figured you wanted it to be kept a secret, but I always knew. You're not only Gramma Carol, you're really Marjorie Ellis."

Henry hugged Mrs Cameron.

She reached down and touched him gently on the shoulder. "No, boy, you're so very clever, but here you've got it wrong. It *is* a picture of Gramma Rachael, Florry, and me. But it's simply the word *me*."

Declan asked, "So you aren't Marjorie Ellis?"

Mrs Cameron nodded her head. "Too many secrets. It's time to tell the truth. I'm not Marjorie Ellis…but my sister is."

Sinclair drew in a quick breath. "Florry? Your sister that's in the home?"

Mrs Cameron nodded.

"All this time you knew where the mysterious Miss Ellis was and you never said anything." Sinclair huffed.

"It was nobody's business. Marjorie Ellis was just a *nom de plume*. She wanted her privacy. She's in Red Deer

Mansion, and she's there because that bloody publisher of hers pushed her into a complete breakdown. She never got better. At least the Heart's Shadow Foundation had the decency to keep paying her royalties which cover the cost of her care, but it's a pittance compared to what they've made over the years."

"How did you end up here?" Charlie asked.

"I saw the housekeeping job advertised by the foundation. I did everything I could to ensure I got the position which gave me a home, a paycheque and a way to watch over my sister's legacy."

Henry pulled away from Mrs Cameron and began pacing around the kitchen. "But, Gramma Carol, you *have* to be Marjorie Ellis. You *have* to be!"

He started to cry.

"Henry. What's wrong? Tell me," she said.

"I'm a horrible person. I've done something really, really bad. Everyone will hate me because I'm so..." His voice was lost in uncontrollable sobbing.

Mrs Cameron rushed to him, knelt down and held him by the shoulders. "Henry. Tell us what's wrong."

"Mr Tull said a lot of nasty things about you and Marjorie Ellis. He shouldn't have been talking about her like that and saying all those bad things about her writing!" Tears streamed down Henry's face.

"What did Mr Tull say?" Declan pushed.

"He said horrible things about her books. He was planning on ruining them so no one would write any more of them, and that wasn't right! He was going to ruin the legacy of Marjorie Ellis. I thought it was Gramma Carol. He had no right!" Henry yelled. He turned to his Gramma Carol. "I had to protect you."

The boy clenched his hands like he was about to punch someone.

"Henry," Declan said in a calm, quiet voice, "tell me what you did."

"I can get into the walls. There's passageways in there, just like the secret panel up to the tower. I could spy on Mr Tull in the writing room, and see Gramma Carol in the kitchen and I could even see into some of the rooms upstairs. That's how I found out where Mr Tull kept his pills. And one night when he was down in the writing room, I snuck into his room and I took some from the bottle. I wanted to stop him.

"And then on the night before Mr Tull died, I was out watching the stars, and Gramma Carol asked me to take him in his tonic. He'd been so mean that day. So I crushed up the pills and mixed them into his nighttime drink. I wanted him gone. Forever!"

Henry started to shake.

"Once I'd given it to him and got back to the kitchen, I knew I'd done something horrible, so I ran back to the room to get it away from him, but he'd already drunk it down. He yelled at me, so I ran."

The story poured out of Henry. "I was scared. So I prayed to my mom and asked her what I should do. I told her I was so sorry and asked her to help me. She's in Heaven now and she should have been able to help me. She could ask God to help me but...she didn't answer. She's always answered me when I talked to her," he said through tears, "but this time she didn't. I thought I'd been so bad that she didn't love me anymore. Or maybe God had kicked her out of Heaven because of what I did. She's being punished because I'm such a terrible person. I was scared, so I decided to pretend like I'd never done it."

Mrs Cameron held him tightly. "You should have said something."

Henry looked up. "It was just another secret. I did it for you...to protect you. But I can't keep it a secret anymore. I did it. I killed Mr Tull."

Chapter Twenty-Eight

Mrs Cameron held onto the sobbing boy. Sinclair stood across from them, arms folded and eyes wide. Declan thought Sinclair might be trying to figure out what his future held, now that it was so tightly linked to these people, the youngest of which had just confessed to murder. Charlie had a strange expression on his face which was impossible to read.

What a fucking mess.

Charlie sniffed the air. "Can you smell that?"

Declan inhaled. There it was. The faint smell of smoke.

"What's wrong?" Mrs Cameron asked.

"Okay, everyone stay put," Declan said.

Declan moved towards the hallway. The smell was stronger. He got to the cellar door and there was no doubt. He placed the back of his hand on the door. Nothing. No heat. Declan carefully opened the cellar door. The air was hazy. He began to make his way down the cellar steps, then partway down, he saw a strange orange glow reflecting on the ceiling above the shelving on the far wall...the shelves that hid the entrance to the tunnel.

"Shit."

Choking smoke rolled over the shelves and started filling the upper part of the cellar. The house was on fire.

Declan ran back to the kitchen as quickly as he could, slamming the cellar door behind him. "Everybody out. Now!"

Charlie ran for the back door, but it was sealed with plywood. "Front door," he yelled.

Declan led the others down the hall, out through the front door and onto the drive.

As they reached the car, he noticed that someone was missing. "Shit! Where's Henry?"

"He was here a second ago," Charlie said.

Declan stared at the house then barked out his orders. "You three, stay put. Charlie, call the fire department and the police. Keep your eyes peeled for anyone out there. I don't think this is an accident."

Mrs Cameron called out, "Henry!" and began running towards the house. Declan grabbed her.

"Don't do it. I'll get him."

Charlie took hold of Mrs Cameron's arm. "Declan will find him. I promise." Mrs Cameron and Charlie joined Sinclair beside the car.

Declan ran back into the house and started calling out Henry's name as loudly as he could. The smoke was dense. It now poured from the cellar door, and from the main room at the front.

"Henry!" he screamed.

Declan considered where Henry might have gone, and focused on the stairs to the second floor. He knew he didn't have a lot of time. The house was nothing but dry wood. It wouldn't be long until—

He stepped on the lowest stair and bounced with all his weight. It hadn't been weakened too much yet. He took another step. There was a loud crash. He turned in time to hear the windows of one of the front rooms blow outward with a force that likely meant that the floor on the other side had given way and the heat had risen into the room at speed.

He looked back up the stairs and made out the silhouette of Henry coming down the stairs draped in a thick blanket and carrying a small suitcase.

Thank God.

"Henry, what the fuck are you doing? We have to move fast."

Before Henry could make it to the bottom of the stairs, Declan swept him up in his arms and jumped to the main floor just as the stair wall started to buckle inward.

Declan launched himself out of the front door. His mass, combined with Henry in his arms, carried them through the porch railing. Declan spun his body to protect Henry from the fall. They landed with the boy on top and Declan had the wind knocked out of him. As he struggled to get his breath back, he saw the tower of the house was now completely engulfed in flames.

"Come on, Henry," Declan heard Charlie's voice say as the weight of the teen was dragged off of him. "You too. Come on."

He felt Charlie's hand in his, pulling him up.

"God," Charlie said. "Either you have to lose some weight, or I have to start working out."

Declan, Charlie and Henry ran from the house. Charlie led them to safety behind the Beast where they joined Mrs Cameron and Sinclair.

Mrs Cameron leapt to her feet and grabbed Henry up in her arms.

"Oh my God, I didn't think I was ever going to see you again." She and Henry were both in tears. She rocked the teen back and forth, petting his hair. Mrs Cameron turned to Declan. "Thank you," was all she could get out.

Sinclair sat on the ground, his back to the car, his arms wrapped around his knees. All four of them joined Sinclair on the ground.

Charlie looked at Declan and said, "I called nine-one-one. Fire and police are on their way."

"Good."

Charlie reached up and brushed the hair out of Declan's eyes. "Are you all right? Can you breathe okay? Are you burned anywhere?"

"I'm fine," Declan said. "Just a few cuts and bruises and I had the wind knocked out of me. For a little guy, Henry sure weighs a lot."

Charlie threw himself at Declan. "I thought I was going to lose you."

Declan pulled him close.

The night sky was lit up by the fire. The flames now rose high above the roof throughout the house. There was a great crash as the remains of the tower fell.

Declan leaned towards Charlie and said quietly, "Whoever started this must be nearby. They'll want to make sure their work's been done right. I need to see if they're still around."

He turned to the others. "I want you all to stay near the car. Understand? If anything threatens you, get in and take off as fast as you can."

They all nodded.

Declan kissed Charlie, then moved away from the car and began to circle the raging inferno.

We might not have made it.

Declan kept his distance from the burning hulk of the building. Then, everything happened at once. A huge man wandered out from around the corner of the burning structure. He was carrying a gas can. There was no doubt about it. It was Adolph Moses.

"Momrath!" a voice behind Declan called out.

He turned to see Henry standing in the light of the fire.

What the —

"Henry! Stay by the —!" Declan was interrupted by a police siren.

Moses looked to see what direction it was coming from. Then he turned towards the four occupants of the house that were now beside the car.

"I'm going to kill you fuckers," he screamed.

A police car sped up the drive then screeched to a halt. Sergeant Bowen leapt out of her cruiser. Moses set down the gas can and reached for something in his pocket.

There was a shot, then Moses stumbled backwards, knocking the gas can over and spilling fuel on his pants. There was a loud crack as the side porch of the house sagged, then collapsed, sending large embers shooting into the air. A cherry-red piece of burning wood landed near Moses, and the flame licked at the gas can beside him. There was a small explosion as what was left in the gas can ignited, heating up the container and sending it shooting into the sky as the air within expanded at a rapid rate. The fire travelled along a path that went from where the gas can had been, directly to the prone man lying on the ground. In an instant, his pants were on fire.

Moses was in flames…at least his lower half was. He began to scream.

"Is that him?" Bowen yelled as she ran to Declan and the others.

"Yes," Declan said.

Out of the corner of his eye, he saw Henry running.

"Henry! Get back here," Charlie yelled. "Fuck!" Charlie went after him.

The boy was headed towards Moses. He was dragging something behind him. It was the blanket that he'd been wrapped in when escaping the house.

Declan went after them both. By the time Declan reached them, Henry had thrown the large woollen blanket over the burning body of his archenemy. The three did their best to beat out the flames.

"Ambulance," Declan yelled out to Bowen.

"On its way," she shouted back.

"Is he the only one here?"

"Not sure," Declan yelled. "Maybe."

Another car arrived on the scene and two officers jumped out of their vehicle.

"You two," Sergeant Bowen called out, "patrol the area around the house to look for any more firebugs. And be careful, this house is going to collapse." Then she turned to Declan, Charlie and Henry. "You have to pull back, too. I don't want any more bodies."

"We can't leave him here," Henry said to Declan, pointing at the burnt man on the ground. "He's still alive."

Declan nodded. "We can use the blanket and drag him to safety."

Moses was moaning and cursing as the three of them struggled to move his huge bulk clear of the heat.

They left him on the blanket beside Sergeant

Bowen's cruiser. A moment later, an ambulance pulled up and two paramedics began tending to his wounds.

Tears streaked Mrs Cameron's face as she yelled, "Henry! You get your butt over here right now!"

Declan followed the boy as he ran to Mrs Cameron and threw his arms around her. Henry looked at her. "I'm sorry we lost our house."

"Not to worry, boy. A house and what's inside it are just things. And you can always get more. What counts is we're all safe." She collected him up again in her arms.

"I have to admit, though, if I had a chance I'd have tried to save a few things..." She stared at the fire.

"Like this," Henry said, retrieving his small suitcase and pulling out the manuscript for *The Ragtag Crew*.

"Now, what the hell are you doing with that?" she said, then engulfed him in another hug.

Henry grinned. "I wanted to protect Miss Ellis' legacy."

Declan frowned. "So that's what you risked your life for?"

Henry shook his head. "Yes. But I also went up for this." He went back into his suitcase, took out a small cigar box and pulled out an old photograph of a young woman. "I needed to save my mom."

Sinclair approached the group and said, "Now about what we were talking about in the kitchen before the fire—"

"Hold on a minute," Charlie interrupted. "Before we discuss Malcolm Tull's death, there's a few things I need to let everyone know. And I need to do this before we talk to the police."

Sergeant Bowen approached them. "Are you folks all right?"

Everyone nodded. Charlie gave her a thumbs-up.

"I'm going to have to get a statement from each of you."

Charlie said, "We've had quite an adventure. If you wouldn't mind, could we do that in the morning?"

"And whereabouts would I find you?" she asked.

Charlie said, "I thought we'd head over to the Rosebud Inn and take rooms there for the night, if that's all right with you."

Sergeant Bowen nodded. "That'll be fine."

After she'd walked away, Charlie looked at them and said, "Sinclair, you can drive over in your own car, and we'll take Mrs Cameron and Henry with us in the Beast."

Declan whispered to Charlie, "What the hell is this all about?"

"Justice," Charlie said.

Chapter Twenty-Nine

They made the short trip from the remains of Hoodoo House to the Rosebud Inn. Declan and Mrs Cameron rode in the back so that Charlie could give Henry his promised ride in the best seat in the Beast. As Charlie parked the car, Sinclair pulled into the lot beside them. Charlie and the others followed Declan as he led the way into the hotel, where they discovered William-Fergus standing at the front desk. He smiled at Declan.

"Good evening, Mr Hunt and…spouse?"

"You guys are married?" Henry whispered to Charlie.

"Long story," he whispered back.

Charlie stepped in front of Declan and took the lead. William-Fergus was wearing a different name tag.

"Good evening, Finn, is it?" Charlie said.

"Yes sir," William-Fergus-Finn replied. "Would you like rooms for the night?"

"I believe we'll need three this evening. One for Mr

Hunt and myself. One for Sinclair Yamada, and another room for Mrs Cameron and Henry if you can manage it."

William-Fergus-Finn looked at the desk log and said, "You're in luck. We can accommodate all of you. We had a cancellation earlier today. Apparently the Ducks Unlimited group had a limited registration for their event, so we have space."

"Excellent," Charlie said. "By the way, Finn, is the dining room closed for the evening?"

"Yes, sir."

"Perfect," Charlie said. "I was wondering if we could use the space to have a bit of a meeting?"

"I think I can arrange that for you."

Declan turned to Charlie with a puzzled look on his face. Charlie smiled and said, "It will all make sense before the night is through."

Once William-Fergus-Finn had checked in the guests, Charlie turned to the others. "If it's all right with everyone, I'd like to meet in the dining room at nine tonight. I have some information I need to share before anyone talks to the police."

Charlie was met with curious looks, but nobody said anything. They simply nodded and headed off to their rooms.

Declan and Charlie's accommodation was the last to be assigned.

"I hope you don't mind, but I've given you the Honeymoon Suite again."

Charlie and Declan looked at each other and smiled. "That would be perfect," Charlie replied. "Thank you."

Declan headed to the stairs, but Charlie stayed behind. He beckoned to William-Fergus-Finn.

"Yes, sir?"

"I'm just curious," Charlie said, pointing at the desk-clerk's badge. "None of those names are yours, are they?"

"No, sir, they are not," he answered, but didn't offer up his real name.

Charlie smiled. Some mysteries were meant to remain unsolved.

He made his way up to the suite where he found the door propped open with a shoe. Charlie entered to find Declan sitting on the couch.

"Where have you been?" Declan asked.

"Trying to solve a mystery."

"What a certain young man's name is?"

"How...?"

"A very top-secret detective trick. It's called eavesdropping from around the corner."

"I see," Charlie said as he plopped himself down beside him.

"So, what secrets do you plan on revealing to us tonight?" Declan asked.

"By 'us' do you mean the Hoodoo House gang when we meet in the dining room, or 'us', as in you and me when we get back up here later?"

"Why do I feel like the latter of those two is going to be far more rewarding?" Declan asked.

"Well, you'll have to wait to see. I don't want to say anything to you until I confirm a few things. It's important I get this right."

"From the devilish grin on your face, I will look forward to both."

"Good," Charlie replied. "Now why don't you go tend to your wounds and leave me alone for a bit while I review my notes."

Declan leaned down and planted a kiss on Charlie's lips, then went into the bathroom.

Charlie spent the next half hour reading his notes and reviewing the photos he had taken on his phone. At just before nine, he called out, "We should get heading down."

They made their way to the dining room and found that a few of the tables had been pushed together to make one larger table. Sinclair, Mrs Cameron and Henry were already there.

A waiter approached. He was William again.

"Good evening, folks. The kitchen is closed, but would you care for any water or drinks while you're having your meeting?"

"I think with the day we've had, a drink would be in order," Sinclair said. "And we'll bill everything to the publisher while we still can. I'll have a double scotch."

"Make that two," Declan said.

"I'll have what they're having," Henry said.

Mrs Cameron intervened. "Make Henry's scotch a warm milk, if you wouldn't mind. And I'll have a sherry."

Charlie ordered a beer.

Once William had dropped off the drinks, Charlie took a sip from his bottle then began. "A lot's happened over the past twenty-four hours and I think it's important that you have all of the details of this case before anyone takes any drastic actions" — he looked at Henry — "like reporting themselves to the police. I have a few questions I'd like to ask.

"Sinclair, I'll start with you. Do you remember the argument you had with Malcolm Tull the night before he died?"

"I do," Sinclair replied, then took a long sip of his drink.

"Do you remember if Mr Tull had been drinking

when you last met?"

"Yes. He wasn't falling down drunk, but he was slurring his words a bit."

"Can you remember anything else about him? Anything physical that was…out of the ordinary?"

Sinclair paused. "He seemed red in the face and in the neck. Sort of…puffy," he said, shrugging his shoulders.

"Did you see any bruising on his neck? Because I recall when we first met, you said the police had noted bruises when they found the body."

"I can't remember precisely, but it is possible. I'd heard through the grapevine," Sinclair continued, "that Malcolm sometimes got involved in rough play with his…friends."

"Do you think the rumours are true?" Charlie asked.

Sinclair stared into Charlie's eyes. "I can guarantee it."

Charlie nodded. "Just one more thing. Do you remember if Mr Tull had any tattoos?"

Sinclair paused before saying, "Why would you ask me?"

"You worked closely with him. I just thought you might notice if he had a tattoo, perhaps on his arm?"

Sinclair squirmed in his seat. "He did have a spider tattoo. I believe it was on his left forearm, but he usually kept it covered with a long-sleeved shirt. But I don't see what that has to do with anything."

"It has to do with something I discovered when looking at some video evidence."

The blood drained from Sinclair's face, but he said nothing.

Charlie turned towards the other end of the table. "Mrs Cameron—do you remember seeing anyone around the house other than Mr Yamada around the time of Malcolm's death?"

She paused. "Bikers. The day before Mr Tull's body was found, I remember seeing a Harley by the side of the house. I never saw the owner, but I knew it was one of his…visitors. And I remember a young man on a motorbike. Not a loud motorbike like the others. It was quieter. That fellow came by on the day they removed Mr Tull's body."

"Was that man the one who burned down the house tonight?"

"It was not. It was someone much smaller in size. I chased him off the property with my rolling pin."

Cody White, Charlie thought.

"I remember him," Henry said. "He was nice."

Charlie continued, "I think I know who that person is and I've interviewed him. Now, I have one more question, and this one's for Henry."

Henry went pale. He set down his milk. Mrs Cameron reached over and held his hand.

"This is important, Henry. Do you remember how many pills you crushed up and put in Mr Tull's drink?"

Henry started fussing with his hands. He looked at Mrs Cameron, then glanced at Declan before returning his gaze to Charlie.

"I crushed up…three pills," he said, slowly. "I couldn't put in too many, 'cause I thought he'd feel the grit in the drink and he wouldn't drink it." Henry looked down. "I had to stop him."

"Thank you, Henry," Charlie said. "Being honest is sometimes hard, and you have to be very brave to tell the truth.

"Now," Charlie continued, "Declan and I visited the RCMP office this afternoon. We managed to have a quick look at Malcolm Tull's file and I got a good look at the coroner's report. It listed the cause of Malcolm Tull's death…and it wasn't due to an overdose of primidone."

Declan looked at him in surprise. Charlie began to think that *not* filling Declan in ahead of time might have been a mistake.

Mrs Cameron grabbed Henry and gave him a hug. The teen stared at Charlie in disbelief.

"Then, if Henry didn't kill him, who or what did?" Sinclair asked.

"Ultimately, the coroner ruled that Malcolm Tull died as a result of aspiration. He choked to death on his own vomit."

"What?" Sinclair said. "That's such a stupid way to go. What an idiot!"

Charlie continued. "The coroner noted that Mr Tull had bruising on his neck. I believe it had to do with the visitor Mr Tull had on the afternoon before he died — Adolph Moses. He'd come by for a sexual encounter, one that involved choking play. I found a video on the computer that seems to confirm this. The choking may have resulted in the bruising the police report noted. The coroner also indicated that Mr Tull's throat was swollen, causing a narrowing of his windpipe — not enough to stop him breathing, but enough to make his throat tighter than usual.

"On the night that you, Sinclair, had the fight with Mr Tull, he had already been drinking. The coroner's report identified a high level of alcohol in his bloodstream. The alcohol in the *kumis* he drank at bedtime might have added to that, although not by much."

Mrs Cameron frowned. "But what does this all mean?"

"I'm getting to that. Now—the primidone. The police had originally looked into the possibility of his death being a suicide, since they found his pill bottle on the desk. The coroner noted that there was an increased level of primidone in his system, but the levels were too low to be the cause of his death. Apparently, even though the *kumis* Mr Tull consumed that night had extra primidone in it, which we now know was added by Henry, it was not a lethal dose. The extra primidone would have just made him very sleepy."

Henry shook his head, "So I didn't kill Mr Tull?"

Charlie continued, "Ultimately, the combination of alcohol and pills caused Malcolm Tull to vomit. Due to the swelling in his throat, he choked, and by sheer chance, inhaled enough vomit to cause his death. Although there were some questions about the origin of the bruising, according to the report I saw, the police are planning on ruling the death accidental."

There were mumbles of disbelief from everyone in the room. Declan reached under the table and grasped Charlie's hand. He looked at Charlie and said, "Great work. Beautiful summary."

Charlie felt a huge weight lift off of his chest.

"But I still gave him the pills," Henry said. "He might not have thrown up if I hadn't given him the pills. I did something horrible." Henry bent over in tears.

"Henry," Charlie said, "there were many factors at play. He might have still thrown up without the pills, and he might still have died." Charlie paused, unsure what else to say.

Declan looked around the table, then asked Henry, "Do you feel badly for what you did?"

Henry looked up. "Yes," he squeaked out. "It's a sin to hurt someone. I'm going to go to hell and burn."

"Did you do what you did because you were concerned about your gramma?"

Henry rubbed his nose on his sleeve. "Yeah."

"And when Momrath was on fire—and this was a person who had attacked you—didn't you risk your own life to save his?"

Henry remained silent, but nodded.

"Where's this all going?" Mrs Cameron asked.

Declan replied, "The police have no evidence that would lead them to believe that Henry was involved. Ultimately it will be up to them, but outside of this room, nobody else knows about the pills Henry put into the drink, and we know it wasn't enough to kill Mr Tull. Under any other circumstances, the only thing that would have happened is Mr Tull would have had a deeper night's sleep."

"If anyone was going to be implicated in Mr Tull's death based on what the police have," Charlie added, "it would be somebody else."

"What do you mean?" Sinclair asked.

"I made copies of some significant files from Mr Tull's laptop before it was stolen—files that included the video I mentioned of Mr Tull in an interaction with Adolph Moses where they were involved in choking play. If the police were to receive a copy of that file from an anonymous source..."

"But he didn't kill Mr Tull," Henry said. "It'd be wrong to say he did!"

"Yes, it would, Henry," Declan said. "But he is a wanted criminal, and he will be charged with the attack on you and the burning down of Hoodoo House. The video wouldn't be enough to charge him with being responsible for Mr Tull's death, but without any other proof, there would be no need to investigate any further."

Henry nodded his head.

"So…a lot of secrets have come out tonight," Declan said. "And a lot of them have caused harm, but some don't have to. Tonight we all have to decide if we want to keep everything we've learned here a secret, or not?"

The group sat in silence. Sinclair and Mrs Cameron both finished off their drinks. Henry looked around nervously from face to face.

"I'm not so sure about this," Sinclair said.

Charlie looked directly at him. "Keep in mind, Sinclair, that among the files we took off the computer, we found the missing manuscript, which we're happy to turn over to you, but we also kept one other file of a more…personal nature. And it would perhaps be better if that file never found its way into the wrong hands."

Sinclair paused for only a second before saying, "I think, for the boy's sake, we should keep the secret."

"Mrs Cameron?" Charlie asked.

Henry looked up at her.

"I think both Henry and I can keep this secret. Isn't that right, Henry?"

Henry nodded.

Declan stood and said, "So we all agree. When we talk to the police tomorrow, there will be no mention of Mr Tull's death, other than what they already know."

Everyone nodded in agreement. Mr Yamada, Mrs Cameron and Henry got up from the table and left the dining room.

Declan looked at Charlie and said, "You did good."

"So why don't I feel better about this?"

Declan shrugged. "Keeping secrets. It's part of the job. Ultimately we do what we do for the greater good. Now let's finish our drinks and go upstairs."

* * * *

Charlie and Declan made their way to their room on the top floor. Charlie flopped on the couch, exhausted. The meeting had taken more out of him than he'd expected.

"You did well down there, you know," Declan said, sitting beside him and patting him on the knee.

"I felt like I was coming across a bit like Miss Marple."

"You were. And there's nothing wrong with that?" Declan replied. "Look at how successful she was."

"Funny."

Charlie slid over and rested his back against Declan's shoulder. He tilted his head and stared up at the ceiling in silence.

"What's wrong?" Declan asked.

"Did we do the right thing? With Henry, I mean."

"In what way?"

Charlie turned around to face him.

"He confessed to trying to kill someone."

"There was no way he would have killed Tull with that dosage. You said it yourself."

"But the intention was there," Charlie continued.

"Look, he showed remorse for what he did. He's young and didn't think things through. Didn't you ever do something stupid when you were a kid that you regretted later?"

"I got caught shoplifting when I was his age and I got grounded for a month. But stealing a chocolate bar is a far cry from trying to kill someone."

Charlie got up and looked out through the window. "What would happen to Henry if the police found out he was involved?"

Declan shrugged. "He'd probably wind up being referred to therapy and possibly could see some charges laid against him. There's a chance he would be assigned to a youth detention facility. The court could deem Mrs Cameron as being incapable of caring for him, given what's happened under her watch. On the whole, I think it's likely the system would do him more harm than good."

"He's a bright kid," Charlie said. "I wish there's a way we could help him. I mean, he's going to have to carry that secret for the rest of his life."

Declan stood up. "I have a thought. How about I give Michael a call? She might be able to talk him through his problems, or at least know someone who can."

Charlie nodded. "Yeah."

Declan tilted his head. "There's still something else bothering you."

"Keeping secrets is hard."

Declan joined Charlie at the window.

"Yup," Declan agreed. "It can be, and if you've got a conscience—which you do—you'll always feel that way about some secrets."

"Why does everything have to be so difficult?" Charlie groaned.

"Keep in mind that if you really want to get into this work, you've got to accept that keeping secrets is part of this business."

"I know," Charlie said.

Charlie faced Declan. "And what about us?"

"Us? I've been giving that some thought."

"And?" Charlie asked.

"I'm *definitely* going to keep you on at the office. Your work on this case was so good that, if you're up to it, I was thinking that the firm could put some resources into getting you your P.I. license."

Charlie's pulse quickened. "Are you kidding? You mean it? We could do that?"

"I think we'd be crazy not to," Declan replied.

"But, wait a minute. That's…that's not what I meant. When I asked about us, I meant…you know…*us*," he said.

The edges of Declan's mouth curled into a slight smile. "You know what you'd be letting yourself in for? I'm not the most stable guy around."

Charlie shrugged. "I'd be willing to try."

"We could maybe take it slow," Declan said, putting his arms around Charlie.

"That would be nice."

"Spend a few more nights together?" Declan said as he kissed Charlie's neck.

"Mm-hmm."

"And see how that feels?" Declan whispered as he nibbled Charlie's ear.

"That feels right." Charlie sighed.

Declan picked Charlie up in his arms, and said, "What do you say we put that king bed to good use?"

"I thought you'd never ask."

Epilogue

Charlie sat at his desk looking at his new screensaver image. It was a picture he had taken the morning after the fire had burned Hoodoo House to the ground. The image showed nothing but a pile of charred timbers, and the soot and ash-covered Spirit of the Hoodoo statue standing proudly against the prairie sky.

That morning, Sergeant Bowen had taken everyone's statement, but her focus had been more on how the fire had started, and if Henry could identify Adolph Moses as the man he had encountered on the night of the break-in. Malcolm Tull's death was never mentioned.

The following day, Charlie had called upon his tech wizardry to anonymously send the video of Adolph Moses with Malcolm Tull to the RCMP. He'd ensured that it was sent through encrypted accounts that couldn't be traced back to him. And to be double-sure, Charlie had imported the file onto a burner phone, sent it from a remote location then destroyed the device.

While the video wasn't meant to be conclusive proof that Moses had been involved in the death of Malcolm Tull, Declan and Charlie had hoped that it would point the police away from Henry's involvement.

One thing Charlie was stumped about was the motivation for Moses' attack on the house. If Moses had known the bikers who had stolen the computer, then he knew it wasn't in the house and he had nothing to gain by burning it down. Charlie could only assume that it had been an act of rage-driven spite after being bested and injured by a kid during the break-in. No matter what, Charlie suspected that Moses was going to be locked away for a very long time.

The door to the office opened and Declan came in with a couple of large coffees and a bag.

"One large latte for you," he said, handing it to Charlie. "And this is from Gwen." He passed Charlie the bag. "She instructed me not to open it. It was for your eyes only. I don't know what spell you've cast over that woman." He shook his head. "So did you get in touch with Cody White?"

Charlie nodded. "I let him know that the files connected to his indiscretion were destroyed and that we haven't kept a back-up copy."

"Good. And our other client?" Declan asked.

"Sinclair has reviewed Tull's last book and decided that it was trash. He said even as erotica, it was a joke. Apparently he's hoping to find work with the publishing company that was in the process of acquiring Mount Temple Press, and maybe trying his hand at writing fiction. He mentioned an idea for a story about a popular romance writer who's gone AWOL and is killing off the ghostwriters that have been hired to finish her work."

Declan grinned. "Nobody would ever believe it. By the way, I just had a call from Mrs Cameron. Mount Temple Press is going to pay her a release settlement which will allow her to start looking for a new home. She's decided that she and Henry will move to Red Deer so she can be closer to her sister. And in other good news, Michael has been in touch with her and has referred Henry to a therapist friend in the area who will take him on as a client."

"Fantastic," Charlie said, raising his latte in a toast.

Declan leaned over and kissed Charlie on the head. "I'll be in my office if you need anything."

Charlie took a sip of his coffee and began to open the mail. On the top of the pile was an envelope from the Heart's Shadow Foundation containing a cheque to cover the expenses of Declan Hunt Investigations. Charlie looked more closely at the cheque and laughed.

He poked his nose into Declan's office. "You'll be glad to know that the cheque's in from Heart's Shadow and it should cover the rest of the month's expenses. I'll deposit it after lunch."

"Great. Thanks."

"Oh," Charlie continued, "you'll never guess who signed it."

Declan shrugged. "No idea."

"None other than the accountant on the foundation board...our very own Palvinder Attwal."

Declan shook his head. "How many pies does that man have his fingers in? Do me a favour. Send him a note thanking him for processing the payment so promptly."

"Will do," Charlie said, turning to leave.

"How is it that you didn't pick up on his connection to all of this?" Declan asked.

It was Charlie's turn to shrug. "I guess I just never got around to checking into who was on the board," he said sheepishly.

"Maybe you're not ready to go for your P.I. licence after all?" Declan teased.

Charlie grinned. "Bastard!"

"Come here," Declan said, kissing him when he got nearer.

"Isn't that a bit unprofessional? What if a client comes in?"

"They'd have to find someone else to kiss them. How about we close the office early and head upstairs? Up there, what we do is our own little secret."

More secrets.

Charlie pulled away and said, "I still have to get that cheque into the bank and…"

"What's wrong?" Declan asked.

Charlie walked around the desk and plopped himself into a chair. "This whole case has got me thinking. Everyone was keeping secrets—Mrs Cameron and her sister's identity, Tull being a ghostwriter for Marjorie Ellis, Henry and what he did to Mr Tull. Sinclair and Cody were both terrified about what would happen if their private lives ever came out."

"Okay," Declan said as he came around the desk and sat on the edge.

Charlie stared down at the floor. "I know some secrets are important to keep in order to help people. But others…personal ones…they can really eat away at you." He looked at Declan. "I'm tired of doing that. I don't want to keep those secrets anymore."

"Secrets like what?"

"Like the fact I'm gay and I've never had the guts to tell my parents. It's a huge part of my life that they don't know about. "

Charlie took a deep breath. "I also want to be open with them...about us. I know it's early, and it may not last, but I want them to know that I've found someone special and I'm not alone anymore. Would you be all right if I told them?"

Please don't say no.

Declan reached down and took a hold of Charlie's hands and pulled him up into a hug. "I think telling them is the right thing to do, and that includes telling them about me."

Charlie pressed his face into Declan's chest.

"So, when is all of this going to happen?" Declan asked.

"I won't tell them about us right away. Being gay is going to be tough enough for them to process without having to face up to the fact that it's *you* I'm involved with."

"Am I that terrifying?"

Charlie pulled back and looked him in the face. "Yup."

They both sat down.

"Are you going to tell your dad and Gwen about me?" Charlie asked.

Declan paused, then said, "Gwen probably already has an inkling, but yeah, if I'm going into this relationship, I'm going to go all in. I have no idea how my dad will react. Who knows, maybe he'll surprise me? After all, I'll finally have someone responsible in my life."

Charlie was excited. "When are you going to tell them?"

"I'll let you tell your folks first. We need this to be a controlled release of information. So, they have no idea that you're gay?"

"I doubt it. I suspect that since Carrie and I live together, they think *we're* in a relationship. They're probably just waiting for the news of a pending grandchild. They won't be happy. But Gran knows and she's good with it, so she'll be there to talk some sense into them. What will get them more riled up is when I tell him that I'm studying to become a P.I. I can hear my dad now — '*After all that time you spent getting your degree in computers, not to mention all the money your mother and I spent.*'"

Declan stood up. "Are you sure you're ready for this?"

"Yeah. I think so."

Declan pulled a bottle and two glasses out of his desk drawer. He poured healthy servings of scotch into both, and slid one across the desk, then raised his glass and looked Charlie in the eye. "Then let the adventure begin. Here's to us."

Charlie grinned. "To us."

Want to see more from this author?
Here's a taster for you to enjoy!

The Woodcarver's Model
Peter E. Fenton

Excerpt

He closed the door behind him and leaned against it as if his weight would hold out the world. How many of them had there been? When was he going to learn to think before he acted? This time he could have died. His heart raced. Fucking idiot! Where the fuck had Yussuf gone?

Rob woke with a start. From the look on the face of the passenger in seat 2B, Rob must have gasped or yelled. He was breathing heavily. Rob pressed the call button for the flight attendant. There was time for one more gin and tonic before they landed.

Once in the airport, after passing through customs, he retrieved his luggage from the baggage carousel. One large green canvas duffle bag — which looked more like it had been dragged by the plane rather than stored in its cargo hold — was all he had, other than his beaten-up leather shoulder bag. He made it out to the cab stand and took the next available taxi.

"Queen's Quay Terminal building, please," he said to the driver, then closed his eyes. He didn't want to appear to be rude by not talking. *So Canadian*, he thought. The *oh-look-I've-fallen-asleep* ruse usually fended off any attempt at mindless chatter from a driver. And he didn't need to see the sights. The ride from Toronto's Pearson International Airport to his home on the lake shore was nothing to see. It was all highway, industrial complexes, stubby office buildings and shopping malls. The trip showed Toronto as the ugly, unimaginative metropolis that it was, until they hit the expressway by the lake. Then it all changed — the lake, so big that it looked like a sea, the gaudy glamour of the Palais Royale dance hall, and the century-old buildings of the Canadian National Exhibition — they still made Rob smile. A quick left onto Queen's Quay and he was almost home.

During the cab ride, he thought of his last night in Mogadishu. Of returning to his hotel room after dinner with his photographer. The Hotel Mustaqbal on the traffic-jammed Wadada Uganda was one of the better accommodations in this war-torn country. Clean rooms with a fair certainty of hot and cold running water. What else could he have asked for in Somalia?

When he'd entered the room, he had sensed, without even turning on the lights, that everything had been tossed. He'd frozen, not wanting to make a sound in case the intruders were still there. Whoever'd done this was probably looking for his computer, jewellery, identity papers — anything of value. The joke was on them. He'd learned years ago never to travel with electronics, other than his phone, and he kept that and his identification on him at all times. And he wrote everything in notebooks. He never had to worry about notebooks. No one wanted them, they didn't break and they didn't run out of power in a jungle. He'd once lost his pen in Tierra del Fuego but was still able to finish writing using a charred stick from the fire.

As he had surveyed the damage in his hotel room, he'd heard a noise. Out of the corner of his eye, he'd seen a figure make for the window. It was Abdi, his driver. Abdi had thrown himself out the window onto the fire escape. Rob had chased him. Why? He didn't know.

They'd both hit the main street running. Rob had run right past a man leaning against a car talking to someone in front of the hotel. He'd kept going for another few hundred yards before realising it had been his guide, Yussuf. It was a few blocks later, on a small side street, that Abdi had yelled something in Somali to a few men. One had pulled out a gun and started firing at Rob. Rob had been pinned in a doorway, shards of concrete flying all around him, when he'd heard more shouting. More firing. *Where the fuck was Yussuf?* Then there was silence. Finally, a familiar head had poked around the corner.

"It's safe now, boss. You come. Come!" Yussuf had waved him to follow. In his hand, he'd held an old CAR-15 automatic rifle. A body lay in the street. Rob hadn't stopped to see who it was.

Life as an adventure travel writer was not what he thought it would be when he began this job. There was adventure, and there was this. One of these days, the adventure was going to win and all of the Yussufs in the world would not be able to save him.

* * * *

"Just by the water taxi stand, please."

The driver pulled over to the curb. Rob paid the fare, wished him a good day, then toted his bag over to the pier.

The water taxi was a small open boat that ferried passengers from the mainland to one of the Toronto Islands. Formed from sediment washed from the Scarborough Bluffs to the east, the islands had once been a large sandbar which extended as an unbroken spit into the waters of Lake Ontario. Hurricanes in the mid-1800s had severed what were now the islands from the mainland. Over the years, houses, some no more than holiday shacks, had cropped up. Larger homes had followed. SeaBreeze, a modest three-bedroom, two-storey house with a roof deck, had been built in the late 1960s by Rob's parents. They'd seen it as a needed quick-access get-away from their busy urban life. It was now the place Rob called home.

The sign for SeaBreeze, pegged to the front door, had been hand-carved by a local craftsman who'd missed the space after the *Sea*. Rob's parents had found it charming and wouldn't let him re-carve it. Here, Rob was at peace. It was just him, the trees and Lake Ontario. The sounds of waves on the shore and the cries of the birds were the only music he needed. They reminded him of his parents, and they were good memories.

He walked through the front door and everything was as he'd left it. All except for the dishes in the sink and the black bra on the floor under the baby grand piano. He was fine with that. At least, he would be fine with it as soon as he tidied everything up. And as soon as he'd settled in, he would call his cleaner to book an appointment.

As much as Rob thrived on chaos in the field, home had to be…organised. It was his problem, he realised that, but this was his home. Karen, who took care of the place when he was on assignment, was, to put it politely, a slob. *"Look after your house? Of course I don't mind. Why would I? You've seen where I live. Looking after a flophouse would be a step up in the world."* It was because of Karen that he'd bought the piano. He couldn't play a note. It had to be tuned regularly because of the lakefront humidity, but that didn't matter because Karen loved it, and she could play like Billy Joel.

Anyone seeing this house and hearing that the owner was a travel writer might think that writing was quite a profitable venture. SeaBreeze, with its luxurious finishes and lake view, could lead them to that conclusion, but they'd be wrong. Rob Hanson made little money. Some years not enough to cover expenses. This lifestyle was thanks to his parents — structural engineers who'd specialised in large-scale hydroelectric projects. They'd flown down to inspect one of their constructions on the Marañón River in Peru when their plane had gone down. That was twenty years ago.

Rob felt that he'd had a happy childhood. His parents had been his best friends. They'd treated him like an adult from an early age, openly discussing their lives, sharing their fascinations and friends with him. He had always felt safe, comfortable and loved.

He'd been raised by his parents in an old Victorian house on South Drive, in Toronto's Rosedale neighbourhood, one of the city's wealthiest communities. It was the home of the old-time gentry — of merchants, doctors and lawyers, of inheritors of money that no longer seemed to work for a living. The other two most affluent neighbourhoods, Forest Hill and the Bridle Path, were built for a different sort, each with its own...requirements. Rosedale, for instance, was the realm of the old white Anglo-Saxon Protestants. Rumour had it that even during the latter part of the last century, people couldn't purchase there if they were Jewish. The wealthy and well-connected Jews and foreign émigrés established themselves in Forest Hill, an enclave of newer stately homes constructed a little further from the centre of their world — Toronto. The third neighbourhood, the Bridle Path, was for the gaudy nouveau riche — entertainers and entrepreneurial magnates — who desired large mansions and larger properties still within the confines of the metropolis.

Homes on South Drive, like their owners, were on the modest side of wealth. Rob's parents had been accepted there despite their lack of historic connections, by virtue of being *clever people*. A neighbourhood like Rosedale liked clever people. It wore them like a Hermès scarf. Clever people made the other people feel chic and intelligent.

What Rob loved most about South Drive was its proximity to the Moore Park Ravine, a large expanse of wilderness in the city. He'd spent most of his free time there, exploring, making trails even deeper into his own private jungle. Here, his imagination had run wild. Here, he had learned the names of every tree, shrub, animal and fungus. Here, he had taught himself how to photograph everything from the largest tree to the smallest insect. But, more importantly, he'd learned to love, respect and understand nature.

Rob had been in his mid-twenties when he'd heard the news that his parents had gone missing. Their plane had gone down in the Peruvian jungle. When he'd received the news from an old family friend, a company lawyer, there'd been a bit of a disconnect. He'd heard the words, but his mind had only focused on Peru. *That's where Paddington Bear came from. Deepest, darkest Peru. I wonder if they'll meet any bears?* Why a twenty-five-year-old would have that thought had never occurred to him at the time.

He had been flown down to the area by his parents' company during the search. Karen, whom he'd known since university days, had come along for support. Rob's sister, Jessica, thought too young to be involved, had been left in the care of their aunt.

It had taken authorities three weeks to discover the tangled wreckage of his parents' DHC-7. Rob had held Karen's hand as they were flown to the crash site by helicopter. There'd been no sign of human remains left at the site. He and Karen hadn't spoken. They'd clasped hands and focused on breathing. Neither had experienced death up until then.

As he'd stood in the jungle, surrounded by shards of debris, Rob had cried. He'd thought of never seeing his parents again, not knowing if they got out of the plane in time and were still out there…lost. Or had the animals… No, he wouldn't let his mind wander there. But the more he had looked around, the more he'd felt, as inappropriate as it might have seemed, that in some strange way, his parents would have liked this as their final resting place. They'd both loved the wilderness. Rob had stayed on-site for the following week as the search continued, and the longer he stayed, the more peace he'd found. It was there that he had discovered what he wanted to do with his life — explore the wilderness.

When his parents' estate had been settled, including the sale of their company, Rob Hanson discovered that he would never have to fear for his financial future. He'd become one of Toronto's most eligible bachelors.

About the Author

Hoodoo House is Peter E. Fenton's third novel. His first book, *The Woodcarver's Model*, was released in 2022 through Pride Publishing and was a nominee in four categories for the Best of 2022 in the Goodreads M/M Romance Members' Choice Awards.

His second novel. *Mann Hunt*, was the first book in the Declan Hunt Mysteries series and came out in August of 2023. Peter is also published by James Lorimer & Company Ltd. Publishers in Canada, who will be putting out his first youth novel, *Not Not Normal*, this fall.

Peter E. Fenton's previous work was focused on writing for the stage, with award-winning productions of *The Giant's Garden*, *Newfoundland Mary*, and *Bemused* which have played across Canada and the United States. Peter spent many years working in palaeontology in remote locations including the Canadian Rockies, the Northwest Territories and Nunavut.

He currently lives in Toronto, Canada with his partner of more than twenty years. At heart, he is an incredible romantic.

Peter loves to hear from readers. You can find his contact information, website details and author profile page at https://www.firstforromance.com/

PUBLISHING

Sign up for our newsletter and find out about all our romance book releases, eBook sales and promotions, sneak peeks and FREE romance books!